THE PILOT

THE PILOT

CA SOLE

Helifish Books

ISBN: 978-1-9161108-6-1 (Paperback)
ISBN: 978-1-9161108-7-8 (ebook-ePub)
ISBN: 978-1-9161108-8-5 (eBook-mobi Kindle)

British Library Cataloguing in Publication Data
A CIP catalogue record for this book is available from the British Library

I am sincerely grateful to my wife and editors who have provided invaluable input to make this a better book.

Author's Note

The Scott Trilogy is about choice and consequence.

The first book, ***Scott's Choice***, told how CJ Scott emerged as two separate individuals, Jonathan and Cuff, each following a different path through life.

In ***Nature's Justice***, Jonathan and his girlfriend, Gudrun, are running for their lives in Southern Africa as they follow their instincts for adventure.

In this story, ***The Pilot***, Cuff embarks on a more stable career, but trouble seeks him out even though he tries to curb his natural tendency to take risks.

Ideally, this series should be read in order: ***Scott's Choice*** followed by ***Nature's Justice*** and then this sequel, ***The Pilot***. You will understand why when you reach the end.

#

This book is written in British English. If you are used to reading American or another variation of English some of the spelling and punctuation may seem different, but it is not incorrect.

1

Return to Society – April

All thought of finding red-billed choughs on the cliffs fled from the bird watcher's mind as quickly as a startled sparrow. He was fixated on the drama unfolding through his binoculars, which his shaking hands struggled to hold in place. He had not seen how the men came to be in that awful predicament – he'd been too busy scanning the cliffs, enjoying the glorious day.

One man was lying on the rock shelf in front of the hovel, his head and arms over the cliff edge. Another hung vertically, his body arched over the yard of grassy slope above the drop. He clung desperately to the hands that gripped his own. Panicked, his legs kicked wildly in space, a sheer fall to the rocks below him.

The watcher saw the man slipping further downward with

each helpless kick he made. And with every inch he dropped, so he pulled the prone man outwards to the edge. The watcher knew with absolute certainty what was about to happen. He scrabbled blindly for his phone, unable to wrench his eyes from the scene. And when the inevitable did occur, he imagined the scream long before it reached him on the bitter wind.

Cuff lay still on the stone ledge, his arms dangling over the lip. Weakened by the strain, his grip had given way. His fingers, wrists and forearms ached. His mind stayed blank for several minutes while it struggled to absorb what had just occurred, but that last sight of Castle's face contorted into a hideous mask of fear embedded itself in his memory. *He's gone, he's finally gone.* Barry Castle had fallen with a scream of terror which lasted only for the couple of seconds before his body hit the boulders a hundred feet below.

Cuff rose slowly. First to his knees, backing away on all fours from the precipice, before standing. He was a climber; heights didn't normally bother him, but after that experience? Well, he would rather stay away from that particular edge. Something was on the back of his hands. Still slightly dazed, he stared down at his forearms. Trickles of blood were running from the deep gouges dug by Castle's nails as he had clung to the very person whose life he'd tried to end. It took a moment for Cuff to recognise what they were, but, now he had seen them, they stung.

He plodded back to the cliff face which backed the hovel. His water supply over the past few weeks had come from a fissure in the rock. The icy trickle had served well to wash, cook, drink and mix with whisky. Now, he used it to clean the gashes in his arms.

His thoughts were jumbled. His meagre possessions needed to be packed so he could leave the place as soon as possible. But what should he do about Castle? Should he report the death and therefore expose his own identity, or should he creep away unnoticed, stay under the radar for as long as possible? Would he get away with it? If not, would his failure to report be construed as him being guilty of murder? *God, what a mess!*

Slowly and mechanically he gathered his things together: his little camping stove and its matching pan, the sleeping bag, assorted bits of clothing and the remnants of his food supply. As he was packing them into his rucksack, the whir of rotor blades and the roar of turbine engines shattered the reigning peace of the wind and the screeching of gulls.

Outside, the coastguard helicopter was making a tight circuit above the cliffs. Someone must have seen what happened and reported it. The decision had been made for him, his life set on a new course by events beyond his control. He could not hide now: he would have to disclose who he was and what had taken place.

He sat with his back against the cliff. The helicopter winched two men and a stretcher down to the rocks. From where Cuff was, at the end of the ledge where Castle had had him cornered between the cliff and the drop, the body could just be seen. The tide was low, so it was above the water line, but the waves were smashing into the rocks, and the winchmen would surely get soaked from the spray were it not for their protective suits.

The two men strapped the body – Castle had already ceased to be a person to Cuff – into the stretcher and signalled for the hoist operator to lift them back up. One of the winchmen remained on the rocks, waiting his turn. His attention was caught by something, and he stepped carefully from boulder to slippery boulder to reach down to an object which glinted – Castle's long knife.

As the second rescuer ascended past the level where Cuff

was, he gave a questioning up–down motion with his fist. Cuff responded with an unenthusiastic thumbs up. The winchman expertly swung around and went through the helicopter's door. The skill of the crew in conducting such a difficult operation was admirable.

More sobering was that although Cuff's nemesis was dead and out of his life, he could not help but feel depressed. Was there something else he could have done to stop Castle falling? Was it his fault the man was dead?

As he slowly deliberated on what possibilities there might be, two men appeared at the side of the hut. One of them held up a warrant card, while the other was still fishing in his pocket for his own.

For the second time in his young life, Cuff found himself in court. On the first occasion, he had been an essential witness in Barry Castle's rape trial. He had taken part in those proceedings feeling the dwindling effects of concussion, nursing a broken arm and bruised ribs, and had the face of the cage fighter who had lost, all brought about by Castle's sabotaging of his little aeroplane.

This time was different; his damage was temporary and purely mental, and it was only an inquest held in a coroner's court, not a trial. However, the outcome of the inquest would determine whether Castle's death resulted in a trial, so there was a lot riding on it. The judge's place was occupied by the coroner, and there was no jury.

Inquest or not, Cuff searched the room to see who would be for or against him. Martin was easy to spot, with his red hair. He had been a devoted follower since Cuff had protected him from Castle's bullying at school. He had stood by Cuff through some awkward moments with a few minor distortions of the truth and whatever physical support his puny frame could manage. He still limped slightly from the hit-and-run on his bicycle. They had never discovered whether that was deliberate, Castle or his lackeys, or some other cowardly driver. Now, he made his way awkwardly onto a seat at the end of a row. Ginny, the love of Martin's life and the girl who had rescued Cuff from the English Channel in the middle of a storm, was with him. They were his only support, but they could not be of any help.

In contrast, his estranged wife Lisa was there, looking sad and depressed and sitting behind her legal representative. Some difficult questions might come from him.

Castle's mother was obvious. She was sitting alone, three seats away from Lisa. She might try to make things awkward for him as well.

A short, stout man in a tweed jacket was fidgeting nervously. Was he the bird watcher who had seen the accident, perhaps? His evidence would be crucial. There was no one else he could be. Two young, physically active-looking men were joking between themselves before the proceedings started, the paramedic winchmen at a guess. There was also a seasoned man who might be the pathologist or maybe a police officer.

The court stood as the coroner entered. He said good morning to the room and stated that the only purpose of the court was to determine the circumstances of the death, the deceased's identity, where and when he died and how he came about his death.

'It is not the purpose of this court to determine why the person died, nor to apportion blame,' he said and took his seat at the head of the room. This was a great deal less formal than a criminal court, and Cuff's vision of being in the same position as Castle when he was in the dock eased. Nevertheless, things might not take a logical route in his favour. It depended on what the other witnesses said.

The pathologist was called first. He stated with absolute

assurance that death was caused by the fall from the area around the hut to the rocks below, a height of around one hundred feet. There were no knife wounds, he said, and neither did the deceased's clothing show any signs of slashing or puncture. The deceased had fallen on his back, so the front of his clothing was intact, although the grass and earth samples taken from it showed how he had slid over the edge of the cliff outside the hut.

All through the man's statement, Cuff's mouth became drier and drier. The pathologist's monotonous tone produced a black-and-white image as he dragged out every detail of his facts, but the horror of the event was in brilliant colour to Cuff, and he interpreted each one as evidence mounting against him.

He was next to be called and, as the pathologist was evidently reaching the end of his statement, Cuff's heart was clamouring to be released from its cage. With Castle's rape trial, Cuff had not been in the dock, merely a key witness. But this inquest would set a direction for his own future, and he'd been told two possible outcomes were likely: accidental death or unlawful killing. To prove he had killed Castle, someone had to have seen him push the man over the edge, even though he hadn't. It depended on what the bird watcher saw – or thought he saw. *Keep calm.*

He was called. His instinct was to fight any aggressive questions aimed to make him look guilty, but his father's insistence that caution should always override impetuousness nagged him to follow the safest path. Clutching a copy of his statement to the police, he found he had reached the witness box. He affirmed his intention to tell the truth in a voice he didn't recognise, and faced the coroner, shutting out everyone else in the room.

Everyone except Lisa. Her accusing stare would not release him.

As he spoke, his throat gradually lost its tightness and confidence returned. The coroner began his questions. 'You say you tried to prevent Mr Castle falling and you were holding his hands as he dangled over the cliff edge?'

'Yes, sir. I can show you, if I may remove my jacket.'

'Very well.'

A short, whispered conversation at the back of the room was the only sound as Cuff took off his jacket, undid both his shirtsleeves and pulled them up to his elbows. He raised his forearms for the court to see the long, livid scars running down to his wrists. 'Those were caused by Castle clinging on to me as I tried to pull him up. I did not have the strength. Neither did he. His struggling was dragging me outward to the edge. I reached a tipping point: another inch and I would not have been able to stop. It was either he fell or we both fell. I had to let go. His nails sliding down my arms did this.'

The room was silent. The sight of those scars conjured a vivid picture of the scene and carried more weight than his words. He put his jacket back on.

The coroner invited questions for the witness.

Lisa's legal representative stood. He asked a few things which Cuff easily and truthfully fielded, before asking, 'Did you push Mr Castle off the cliff and then have a change of heart?'

'Mr Vine.' The coroner's words were sharp and loud. 'This is an inquest, not a trial. Restrict yourself to questions appropriate to the nature of these proceedings. Mr Scott, you do not have to answer questions which might incriminate you in any way.'

'My apologies, sir,' Vine said and resumed his seat.

The coroner's support boosted Cuff's rising confidence. But Vine had made him angry and thrust a potential hole in his story to the fore. He had to plug it firmly, and his dad's doctrine was not the tool to use.

He gave the solicitor an unwavering glare. 'The answer to your question is no. As I *already* told you: he slipped as a result of trying to stab me and the ensuing struggle. If I had pushed him, why would I then try and save him? Why would I cling on to him as long as I could while I was being pulled to within an inch of my own death? Would *you* try as hard as I did?'

'All right, Mr Scott, you've made you point. You may sit down.'

The coroner was taking witnesses in chronological order, so the next one was the bird watcher. The man, whose name was Miles Twitcher, an association which, to his obvious annoyance, caused a slight stir of amusement in the court, testified that he saw Cuff trying to hold on to Castle and stop him falling. But he added he had not seen how the men had come to be in that position in the first place.

Other witnesses gave statements: one of the winchmen; then Mrs Eva Castle, who, to Cuff's surprise, had a trace of a German accent. She verified the knife did belong to her son, and she did not approve of it.

Afterwards, he stood at the top of the steps outside the court, breathing in cool refreshing air while he waited for Ginny and Martin to join him. The two winchmen trotted down past him. One gave him a sideways look and nodded. What did that mean? Did everyone believe him just because the coroner said it was an accident? Did Mrs Castle believe him? It was important she did; he didn't want her to hold him to blame. Below him, she had reached the pavement and was heading towards a black Mercedes-Benz. Poor woman. She looked to be a pleasant person. How had she ended up with a son like Barry?

Lisa was already at the foot of the steps and beside the car. The rear door of the Mercedes opened and a young woman in a wide-brimmed hat got out. As she held the door open for

Mrs Castle, she glanced up at Cuff. Her face was in shadow and unrecognisable, but there was a hint of fair hair. Another pale head sat on the other side of Eva Castle as she slid into the middle. Lisa opened the front door and got in. She looked tired and dispirited.

Getting through the inquest was one thing; Cuff's confrontation with Lisa was something altogether different. It was intensely personal.

'I don't care if the bloody coroner said it was an accident. He's wrong, they're all wrong, you killed Barry,' she screamed at him. 'You've always hated him and tried everything to destroy him when he was nice to me. You won't hear a good word said about him. You're a bloody bigot. You killed him, and I'm going to prove it. You forced him over the cliff with that horrible knife.'

Cuff struggled to keep his voice calm. If she didn't stop her stupid accusations and admit her faults soon, he was going to yell at her, which would start another bout of weeping. 'Lisa, you heard quite clearly, the only prints on the knife were Castle's. It was his knife. Even his mother said so.'

'You killed him. I don't know how, but I know you did. And now my baby doesn't have a father.' Tears welled in her eyes.

Cuff had seen them flow so easily and so often he was unmoved. 'The coroner ruled it as accidental death, and that's what it was. You know perfectly well I'm not a killer, Lisa. It's not my nature.' His arguments were exhausted. She must accept the verdict and move on. How could he convince her to do that? He simply sat there in his own house in the same seat his father had decreed should be his place in the lounge and watched her, wishing they could conclude this and he could go and get a drink somewhere.

She was wearing black trousers and jacket and a pink

blouse with frills down the front. It suited her with her black hair, always had done. And she knew it, which was why she seldom wore anything else. She was sitting in the ghastly mustard-coloured chair she had bought without consulting him. It had been another point of contention between them. Waiting for her to reply, he glanced around the familiar room. She had hardly changed anything since he left. Even the tired antimacassars were still on his mother's chair, and some of his father's years-old magazines were in a neat pile on the bookcase where they always had been.

'What I don't understand is what you thought you were doing. Why did you try to escape to France? Why did you hide after you were rescued?'

Cuff pulled his sleeves up. 'Lisa, our marriage was never going to work, and certainly not after you reneged on our agreement over kids and slept with Castle. In spite of all that, I was determined to protect you from a bully who was likely to be abusive. To do that, I needed to prevent you from marrying him for as long as I could. If we were to divorce in September after one year, the earliest possible time, then you could marry Castle straight away, and he would have access to everything I would give you in the divorce. I refused to allow him to win all that.

'Instead, if I disappeared, it would take many more months before you could have me presumed dead and the marriage automatically be over. Hopefully, with the extra time, you would come to realise what a thoroughly unpleasant man Castle was. On top of that, you would not be able to benefit from my estate for seven years, so I would also be able to deny Castle my assets for much longer. Knowing that, he might have given up and left you.'

Cuff paused to see if this had sunk in. 'So I decided to disappear and sail to France.' And here he told his only lie; he was never going to admit to pseudocide and incriminate

Ginny and Martin. 'Unfortunately, I capsized and was very lucky to be swept ashore. I set up house in that miserable cottage and decided to lie low for as long as I could.

'I spent weeks in isolation in that hovel, hiding from the world, to win you some protection. Once our marriage was over, I would be able to slink quietly back into society. I wish I could have remained hidden and pretended to be someone else, but for my chosen career as a professional pilot I had to come out into the open at some point. I would have to disclose my true identity before being able to register for the ground training, which is the start of the whole process. I could never do that under an assumed name. I had endless debates with myself on the pros and cons of when to do this, and I still hadn't made up my mind when Castle found me.'

Lisa dabbed a sodden tissue at the tears which trickled down her cheeks. She sniffed and slowly shook her head with a lack of understanding.

Cuff went on. 'He sensed I was alive and came looking for me. You heard the rest at the inquest. He tried to force me to jump over the edge or be knifed into doing so, but he slipped, and I was nearly dragged over with him. You heard what the witness said. I was forced into the open and here I am.'

Lisa was bent forward, her head down, apparently staring at a threadbare patch in the carpet. Rather than go to the expense of replacing the whole thing, his father, Kevin, had covered the area with a cheap Pakistani rug, a copy of an Isfahan carpet, which wasn't there now. Lisa was so despondent she would do nothing about the patch. She couldn't look at him. She sniffed again, her voice quiet and resigned. 'What are you going to do?'

'I want to have a stable and prosperous life with good prospects for rising to the top of the tree. Being in Dad's business was not what I wanted, as you well know. Whatever I choose to do must have variety and, because I love flying,

I've set my sights on becoming an airline pilot. I have the money for the training, thanks to Granddad. It should be a diverse life: different destinations every trip, a whole range of weather conditions to deal with, different aircraft types – all sorts of challenges. It's well paid – once you reach the top end of the scale anyway – and I won't be stuck in the routine of an office or be involved in business.'

'Sounds all right.'

'It could take me two years to get the qualifications to fly large jets, probably more, what with studying and gaining sufficient flight experience.'

Lisa was silent for a while. Having vented her frustrations, she seemed to have calmed down. Should he pity her? Her world had fallen apart, and admittedly he was not being much help. Was she worthy of pity? That was debatable, as this was all her own fault.

'Cuff, do you think we could try again? It would be easy, we're still married.'

He regarded her in silence. This was a core reason why they would never be happy together – one moment she thought of him as a murderer, the next she wanted to resume their marriage. She flipped from one thing to another and back again, unpredictable and indecisive. This meeting was a bloody awful experience, but the decisions which had led to it were sound.

'No, Lisa. I'm sorry, but we've proven conclusively it'll never work. We are poles apart in attitude and outlook. We don't want the same things. To try again would just waste time out of our lives. You need to look to the future and find someone who's more understanding than I am, someone more domesticated.'

'The baby's due in September,' she said, her voice small.

'I know. You have your friend Sheila and your mum and dad. Will Mrs Castle support you? Emotionally, I mean.'

'Yes, I think so. We've become friends.'

'That's good. By the way, who were those young women in the car after the inquest?'

'They are Eva's nieces. They were over from Germany to help her.'

'Oh. Lisa, you have a company of your own, so you have a reasonable income, and you have this house of mine and everything in it until you find someone else to look after you. I'm not clear what else I need to do.' Cuff paused, staring at his wife for a long moment. 'I'll tell you what I will do. We can postpone the divorce until after your baby's born and you've settled down to a routine – but no later than November. I'm not having this dragging on forever. We both need to move on with new lives, and the sooner the better.'

He could not concentrate on driving when he left. *Has Lisa really come to terms with the situation? She seems to have recognised she has to do something positive instead of brooding on her misfortunes. Hopefully, I'll only have to deal with her again over the divorce.*

2

June – Fourteen Months Later

Not wanting to waste any time, Cuff knuckled down and buried his head in the books for ten months, doing little else but study and fly for pleasure. With the exams out of the way, his focus was on increasing his flight experience. So he took the popular route of becoming an instructor to broaden his knowledge and qualifications and have a small income while his hours accumulated.

Terry, who was Martin's father and the airline captain who had taught both boys to fly, was happy to assist in his training. He was vastly experienced and had always passed on his extensive knowledge to Cuff, which gave the young man an exceptionally solid grounding in aviation.

'Once I've got my instructor's rating, I'm going to apply for a post at the Casewell school. It'll be good to teach where I learned, and there's people I know there,' he said to Martin. But when the time came, there were no vacancies at Casewell.

'There's a slot at Fernbury,' Terry told him. 'It's only twelve miles away. I'll have a word with the chief instructor. You'll find Connor a bit different from others you've met. He's ex-RAF and a stickler for standards and discipline, which is a good thing: you can't be weak in that area when safety is at stake. He's pleasant enough, a bit pompous, and he tends to regard civilians as an inferior species, but I'm sure you'll get on just fine.'

'It'll be great. Thanks, Terry. It's a pity I won't be at my 'home' airfield, but I'll be back to hone my aerobatic skills as often as I can.'

Cuff's interview with Connor Royle was unnerving. The school's owner was not a big man at about five foot nine, but he had a lean, weathered and droopy-jowled face. His hair was showing the first signs of grey, and his pale-brown eyes bored into Cuff's as he gave his answers. The questions were phrased as if much more explanation was required than the simple response which was immediately apparent, leaving Cuff searching for the root of each one, or fail. Relief followed when, without comment on the interview, Connor sprang to his feet and said they should go and take an acceptance flight. Cuff, it appeared, had passed the verbal test. He wasn't worried about the flight, but was wary of being complacent and over-confident. He followed Connor out to the aircraft and noticed how light on his feet the chief instructor was; it wasn't an asset which sprang to mind on first meeting the man.

'Take a seat,' Connor ordered when they returned to his office two hours later. 'There's a few things I'd like you to do a little differently. There's nothing wrong with your technique – your handling's rather good, actually – but your whole approach doesn't entirely fit with the school standards.' He moved a neatly stacked pile of papers to one side of his desk and put his notepad and pencil in front of him, taking the trouble to see that it was precisely aligned with the stack.

After the debriefing, the deep laugh lines in Connor's face twisted outwards. The man was apparently smiling for the first time.

'I'll allocate two students to you. That'll be enough for now, but you'll also have to do ground lectures. I'll work you into the programme by tomorrow morning. You'll have to check it out. What you need to bear in mind is there are no weekends as such here. Some of our students have regular employment and can only fly on weekends; others, who are in the minority, don't have a job for whatever reason and can fly at any time during the week. I maintain a programme which conforms to those choices. As an instructor, your off days will not necessarily be over the weekend. In fact, they most often will not be.

'The students themselves are mostly in their late teens or early twenties. As such they are impressionable, so it's important the information they get is factual, truthful and only as much as is needed. Clear?'

He pushed a card file across the desk. 'Have a read of that. It's the school rules and regulations and tells you about the uniform instructors must wear. White shirt, navy trousers and epaulettes depicting your seniority. You get one bar only at this stage.'

That made sure Cuff knew his place in the hierarchy.

'Business aside,' Connor continued, 'we're having our fifteenth-anniversary party on Saturday; all instructors and students should be coming. It'll give you a chance to meet everyone on social terms. Meanwhile, let's go and see who's here, and I'll introduce you. Some are flying, of course.'

Cuff stood and opened the office door to let Connor out ahead of him. The door had a window in it which was large enough for the chief instructor to see out and watch what was going on in the communal crew room beyond, where both instructors and students were able to relax.

A lanky young man in his mid twenties with thick blond hair was stooped over a young woman who was backed against the table in a weak effort not to be dominated. Connor tapped him on the shoulder, and he straightened up. The girl took advantage of the respite and followed suit.

'Craig, this is Cuff Scott. He's joined us as of today. Apart from being an instructor, Craig is the school safety officer.'

'Welcome,' said Craig, flashing a genuine smile. 'You'll enjoy it here.'

Cuff nodded, grinning in response, but before he could reply Connor pulled him on to meet Mike Penny. Connor glanced around the room and could not see anyone else, so he left Cuff with Mike and went back to his office.

Mike had two bars on his shoulders. He was good looking, but short, with a cocky air about him. 'Hi,' he said. 'Yah new to instructing? No problem, I can help yah out on any subject. Don't be scared to ask, respect us what's more experienced, and yer'll get along fine.' He turned away to talk to someone else.

How senior does an extra bar make him?

Tonight is warm and clear with a full moon. The light is streaming in at her sitting-room window, picking out every detail: the table with a bottle of wine, white, a Sancerre, with a single glass; beside it a book – it's too flat to see what it is; in the background a Nespresso machine, a bowl of oranges, a jar of what looks like pasta, and a rag doll. What memories does that special creature hold for her?

It's comfortable sitting here, the conditions perfect. It's quiet with a light, cooling breeze. I can see the road and all the flats around. Late-nighters cross lit windows oblivious to my watching eye. Some lights are already out, the curtains and windows of early-risers open for the air. I am master of it all, and therefore entitled to study her life through my lens.

She has not yet gone to sleep. Her bedroom curtains are closed, the light is on and every now and again there is movement. I could go mad imagining what she's doing.

My God! She's there in the lounge. Oh my God, I am blessed to witness this. My fingers tremble. Control! This needs a steady hand.

Cuff was reluctant to arrive at the party on time. As a newcomer, he wanted to stand back initially and observe. He walked from his flat taking in the evening air, still warm from a hot day, and hoping Mike Penny was not the only person he would recognise.

The lounge area or, as most enthusiasts called it, the crew room, was quite large for a small organisation. Immediately inside the front door was a reception desk, and another door led out to a short lawn and the airfield. Connor Royle's office overlooked it from one side, as did two briefing rooms and a larger classroom on the other. Another office was set aside for flight planning and the aircraft technical documents. A weird collection of unmatched chairs was available, the most comfortable of which was the seat which everyone fought hard to get to first. Cuff later learned some people were particularly anal about claiming that chair.

A pretty girl in a black top with broad white edging was sitting there. A black velvet choker clasped her neck. She stood out in sharp contrast to all the others in their fashionably tatty jeans and T-shirts. Leaning over her in his characteristic manner was Craig with a beer in his hand. On the far side of the room a trestle table had been laid with snacks and finger food, no doubt to absorb the anticipated alcohol consumption. The drinks table was nearby. With one hand on it was Mike Penny talking to a couple of lads;

probably students. Cuff knew no one else, so he went over to Craig to say hello. The slight and amused smile the rangy man was showing to the girl broadened at the sight of Cuff.

'Ah! Imogen, this is Cuff. He's the new boy around here, not that I'm yet an established part of the furniture. I don't know the first thing about him, but he strikes me as being a good bloke.'

Cuff laughed. 'Well, that makes two of us of like mind, at least. Hello, Imogen.'

'Hi. I've only been here a month myself. Just sixteen hours flying so far,' she said, transferring her glass of wine from right to left, and held out her hand. Cuff took it and looked into a pair of impenetrable dark-brown eyes. Her hair was auburn, a little off the shoulder and deliberately shaggy. A mere hint of a delicate perfume hung in the air. Cuff was captivated. Seconds passed. Without realising it, he had neither dropped his gaze nor released her hand.

Craig broke the spell. 'Well, er, I'll just get another drink. How about you?'

Cuff was embarrassed and released Imogen's hand immediately. He pulled his sleeves up, which exposed the livid scars. 'Yes, a beer as well, please.' Turning back to her, he muttered, 'I'm sorry, I didn't mean …'

Whatever she was going to reply was stifled. Mike Penny was striding towards them, pushing his five-foot six-inch frame between groups without apology. He held out his hand to help Imogen up. 'Imo, come. Time to eat.'

Imogen ignored his support but stood.

To Cuff, Mike thrust his chin out. 'Mine. Got it?'

As she walked away behind Mike, Imogen gave Cuff a quick backward glance and a slight smile.

Craig reappeared with the beers. He inclined his head in Mike's direction. 'Bloke's a little prick with small man's disease. Have you met anyone else? Come on, I'll give you an introductory tour. There's Sonia, the woman who looks like she hasn't washed her hair in a month – she's our senior instructor. She's a bit like Connor, actually – very experienced, but no sense of fun. She's got some kind of chip on her shoulder, I don't know what about. She's okay really, won't do you any harm and will give good advice if you ask for it. Don't expect her to offer it, though. See that tubby chap over there? That's Jimmy. He always looks like that, as if he's just got out of bed. Hair all over the place and a bit gormless. Jimmy's okay, funny – amusing, I mean.

'You'll discover Connor is very rank conscious. You and I are the bottom feeders with only one bar on our shoulders, Mike has two, Jimmy has three and Sonia and Connor have four. I don't know what gets you promoted, but Mike is desperate to add more weight to his shoulders.'

'What's with Imogen and Mike?'

'He's her instructor, and he seems to have claimed her as a girlfriend as well. He's very possessive over her, anyway.'

Craig saw another female student and drifted away. Cuff went to find something to eat.

'You must be Cuff.' The voice behind him had a Lancashire accent and came from well below his shoulder. He turned to see Sonia. She was pushing forty and had a long, chiselled, almost masculine face. There was an athletic quality to her, thin and sinewy in her blue tracksuit bottoms and black sleeveless vest. As Craig had pointed out, she was unkempt, and her hair was lank. Cuff smiled at her, but she didn't return the gesture. She took two small triangular sandwiches, put them on her paper plate and said, 'Where did you learn to fly, then?'

'Over at Casewell. I've a good friend whose dad is a 747 captain. He taught me, and taught me aerobatics as well. It's become my passion.'

'Aerobatics, eh?' Sonia's long face split into a grin. Cuff

had heard she seldom had more than a sour expression, so was pleased.

'We must have a discussion about that sometime. I used to do a lot and was told I was rather good.' Her eyes twinkled at the memory.

'Perhaps we could go up together? I'd love to have the benefit of your experience. I can get an aircraft at Casewell.'

Sonia nodded slowly; that slight smile again. 'We'll do that.'

Connor strode across the room to interrupt, his voice curt. 'Sonia, the white wine's short.'

She ignored him, although a flicker of annoyance crossed her face. After what was obviously a deliberate delay, she drained her glass in one gulp, glanced briefly at Cuff and went off to resupply the bar.

Cuff took a deep slug of beer as he watched her. Connor's order was actually quite rude. *There are some curious undercurrents in this place.*

Imogen tidied her flat before going out. Somehow, making the bed, putting things away and cleaning a small section every day set her up for whatever lay ahead. It was nine thirty and time to leave for the airfield. She took her jacket off the rack, put on her trainers and opened the front door.

A bunch of flowers lay there. Red and yellow roses, cerise and purple stocks and two types of flowers she couldn't identify; lilac and purple, anyway. There was a note. Without picking up the bunch, she read, *To my beautiful, lovely lady. Without you I am nothing.* There was no signature.

Who? She flipped through the men currently in her life: *Mike, not his style; Craig, possibly, he fancies me; that new man, Cuff, the way he held my eyes the other night? It could be him.*

Puzzled, but sufficiently pleased to smile to herself, Imogen took the flowers into the kitchen and put them in a bowl of water. She didn't have a vase. Outside again, she unlocked her bike and set off for the airfield.

She is a goddess, Aphrodite, the personification of beauty, pleasure, love and procreation. Her skin as smooth as silk. Her hair, a delightful thick auburn, deliberately tousled so as to express her sense of fun. She is merry, her laugh infectious, her movements sometimes quick, sometimes fluid, always sensual. When she looks at me her eyes entice and flirt, the flame within them dancing in open invitation.

She will be pleased. She'll be curious. She'll wonder who I am, who it is that appreciates the wonder of her form and personality. My heart craves her. I just want to give her so much that she cannot help but trust me. And when I finally reveal myself she will be so overcome by my generosity and admiration, she'll fall into my arms.

Cuff quickly settled into the routine. He was not as busy as he would have liked; but his work was dependent on the availability of his students, one of whom wanted to fly all day, every day, and the other who had so many other commitments he only appeared once a week, if that. To Cuff, they were decent enough people, but not likely to be friends.

Craig was proving to be a genuine ally, who was always looking for someone as an anchor in his life. He either held or organised others to hold parties to which Cuff became a regular invitee. But Cuff found them to be too much of the same old thing after a while and became more selective about which ones to go to.

At one of the earlier ones he noticed Imogen with Mike. She appeared tense. He was gripping her wrist, not holding her hand.

Cuff had already tired of Mike's assertion of his assumed authority in the school. The man could not help throwing his weight around and passing opinions on all matters aviation, much of which Cuff knew to be wrong or at least inaccurate. At work he refrained from comment, but here the urge to poke the little man's ego was too difficult to resist.

Mike had his back to him. Imogen was studying him as he approached. Was that a welcoming expression he saw?

'Imogen, would you like to dance?'

Mike spun round, his grip still on her wrist. 'No she wouldn't. We're talking.'

Cuff did not take his eyes from hers over Mike's head. She was clearly amused, but she shook her head.

He left and went to join Craig, who was talking to a pretty blonde girl Cuff hadn't seen before.

'Cuff! This delightful creature is Hannah – I think. She's German and has an identical twin sister somewhere.' Craig's face was an open book. Orgies were for fantasy in Cuff's mind. Having sex in the company of other men wasn't appealing.

Hannah showed no sign that she understood. 'Hello.'

Craig spotted the twin and beckoned her over.

'Hello, I'm Anna.'

They stood shoulder to shoulder, two identical pretty faces, two identical fair pixie cuts, four identical blue eyes, two pairs of jeans with the same ripped knees and four small red shoes lined up in a row.

'I'm already confused. Don't swap positions whatever you do. You're identical, aren't you?'

As the party became more lively, the twins showed no inclination to circulate and politely refused Craig's invitation to dance.

'Cuff, let us eat something,' said one, and tugged at his right arm.

'Yes, I'm hungry also,' said the other, and pulled at his left.

Craig said, 'I'll get some drinks. Same again?'

'Please,' Cuff replied and followed the twins to the food.

Craig shrugged, got the drinks and went to search for better luck elsewhere.

After midnight the crowd dwindled.

'We are told it is very safe here, but we are not familiar with UK and a little nervous, actually. Will you take us home, Cuff, please?'

Imogen was watching them as he and the twins put on their jackets. Was it his imagination, or was there a look of disapproval on her face? Or was it disappointment? He had never even had a full conversation with her, yet he now had an unreasonable sense of guilt.

Hannah clung to his right arm, Anna to his left, as they trod the wet pavements.

'Where do you live, Cuff?'

'Down the next street.'

'Let's go and see.'

'It's late, and my place is in a mess. Another time?'

'We live in a mess, too. There is no shame. Come, you can give us coffee and maybe some schnapps, no?'

'Coffee yes, schnapps, no. Sorry.'

A quarter to five. The sun was up, although not yet visible from the window of his flat. One twin slept at his left shoulder, one at his right. He had no idea which was which.

What a night! How the hell did that happen? I didn't ask for it – I didn't even flirt with them. Whatever. It was good to blow off some testosterone, and I needed it.

Later, Cuff was to meet Martin and Ginny at The Gargoyle for lunch. Weaving its way into the conversation would be Ginny's advice on how he should live his life. It was her way of trying to help, and he treated her words with respect and a little humour. In her view, as Martin's close friend he was someone to be looked after, and her advice was genuinely meant to ensure his safety and well-being. But the main reason she took an interest was to supervise his activities to ensure he did not expose her own man to danger; something he had previously been inclined to do.

Ginny and Martin had obviously been conspiring over him, because when they met, his friend said, 'You've been leading an ordinary and unexciting life since you took this job, Cuff. Did your little survival exercise bring you down to earth, shock you a bit?'

'No. I made a decision, I chose a path to a career and I'm trying to follow it through. I have to admit there's something missing in my life, though.'

'You don't have a girlfriend, Cuff.'

'No, Ginny, it's not that. Things are progressing okay professionally, and they can't go any faster, but I lack excitement.'

'You know,' Martin said, 'you're incredible. You felt you had to make a choice between a life of adventure and one of stability. Instead of following your instincts, you chose stability, and it turned into a can of worms. You married, drowned in the misery of your business and got divorced. The last time we saw you with a spark in your eye was when you survived that capsize in a raging storm – thanks to Ginny.'

'You're right. I know you are. I should have followed my instincts instead of taking Dad's advice to settle down. I keep thinking how we're the product of our genes, modified by upbringing, education and experience, but our natural tendencies cannot be changed. In pursuit of my career I've tried to push my instincts behind me, but it's not working. I miss the thrill of the kiss of danger.'

Ginny seized on the opportunity to analyse. 'So, what would you be doing if you'd made the other choice? You'd have an alter ego. Now what you need to do is put yourself in his position. Let's give him a name – we'll use Jonathan, your middle name. Keep asking yourself what 'Jonathan' would do in situations. But better still, revert to what you were, *be* a 'Jonathan', follow your instincts when making decisions, don't dissect everything. You were acting as 'Jonathan' when you pretended to cross the Channel, so those tendencies are still there inside you. You've been indoctrinated with a desire for a conventional life. You need to remove that from your mindset and do whatever makes you comfortable. There's no need to change your career, and you'll be much happier.'

Cuff thought about that for a moment. 'Again you're right. Thanks, I think I knew that, but needed confirmation.'

'Now, about this missing girlfriend …'

Cuff was not going to admit to the German twins, even to his good friends. It would be embarrassing, although he was not sure why. *'Jonathan' wouldn't be embarrassed, would he?*

'I've met a few girls in the months since the divorce, but every time I meet someone I like and respect, I avoid going any further. I'm not in the mood for a relationship at the moment, and I know it's because of my experience with Lisa. She's made me very wary. Her lies, her instability, her jealousy and the fact that she deliberately and sneakily breached our agreement has left me reluctant to trust anyone. This attitude will fade eventually, I suppose – I hope. Until then I'll be keeping my distance. I don't know what the hell I want, Ginny, and quite frankly it's not something which worries me. Having said that, there's a student who I think I've clicked with. She seems really nice and might be responsive if I approached her.'

Martin interrupted. 'So why don't you? Ask her, I mean?'

'Because she's already going out with one of the other instructors, and to interfere would cause ructions in the school. Man's a jerk, actually; I can't understand what she sees in him.'

'What's the matter with him?'

'He's short—'

'I'm short, you peasant. It's not a crime.'

Cuff laughed. 'No, but he's got a serious case of small man's syndrome. He's nauseatingly self-opinionated and seeks attention all the time. The instructors ignore him mostly, but the younger students, who are more impressionable, see a good-looking, smart, athletic, charming and humorous bloke who works out and has a vast amount of knowledge – as he keeps telling them. They hang on his professional pontifications about how to fly advanced manoeuvres, most of which is bullshit anyway.'

'He doesn't sound like a good match for your 'really nice' girl.'

'I don't know the ins and outs of it, and I'm not going to interfere.'

3

01–07 July

A refreshments counter stood opposite the reception desk near the main entrance to the crew room. Stocked with tea and instant coffee as well as an espresso machine, it was a popular gathering point. Standing there, it was possible to see into all the briefing and lecture rooms and Connor's office through their door windows.

First thing in the morning, before their students arrived, Cuff and Craig were serving themselves espressos. Cuff looked up when Jimmy came through the entrance with an eager expression on his face. Before even picking a cup, he tugged at their sleeves and pulled them into a tight, confidential group. Mike Penny was standing apart, but he noticed and came over to listen to the gossip.

'You're not going to believe this,' Jimmy said. 'On Saturday evening, I went out to dinner with my brother and his girlfriend – woof, woof! If he wasn't my brother, I'd have a serious go at her. That's one very hot lady. Anyway, that's not the news. We went to the Squire's Arms. You know, that fancy country hotel out the other side of Pangbourne.'

'Yeah, I know it. It's expensive, but it has bloody good food.' Craig smacked his lips.

'That's it. The hot news is, as we came out of the dining room, there were Connor and Sonia, standing at reception! Now, I'm not saying they were checking in, but what else could they be doing when there were two overnight bags on the floor?'

'Connor and Sonia? Really?' Craig squinted at Jimmy. 'This isn't one of your daft jokes, is it? Because if it isn't true, it's cruel and damaging.'

'No, no. I may joke, but I won't be nasty. This was true – honest.'

'Well, good on them,' said Cuff. 'Why shouldn't they have an affair? It's a free world and they're both single. I don't blame them for hiding it from the public eye, especially us, do you?'

Jimmy nodded, but it was Mike who responded. 'I don't get what those two see in each other. Connor's a miserable sod and so is she, and she's a face like an 'orse.'

Craig leaned over his shorter colleague. 'Stop being a bloody chauvinist, Mike. Sonia has a bloody good little body. She's fit, too, and is actually a nice person if you treat her with respect. She can't help what she looks like, and maybe Connor is big enough to appreciate her character ahead of her looks.'

Mike sneered. 'If she showered and washed 'er 'air it would 'elp.'

'But haven't you noticed how Connor treats her like dirt most of the time?' Cuff said. 'How is that compatible with spending a weekend away with her?'

'No idea, Cuff. Except maybe she enjoys being dominated.' Jimmy laughed.

Craig waved a finger at him. 'Oh, bull, Jimmy. Stop thinking the worst of people.'

Jimmy scratched his tousled hair. 'Sonia hasn't two beans to rub together, or so she claims. Supporting her mother and so on. If that's true, then Connor is paying for the hotel and everything that goes with it.'

'You're not suggesting he's paying her, are you?'

'No, not at all. I told you, I'm not unkind. I'm just saying Sonia is skint and therefore Connor's paying.'

Imogen topped up Melissa's wineglass. 'How are your furry creatures?'

'They're all on the mend, except a hedgehog, which was brought in this morning. Poor little chap's been hit by a car. The vet's not sure if he'll make it – he may do. We're all holding thumbs.'

'That's sad.' Imogen pointed to her counter-top. 'The other day, the day after the school party, someone left a bunch of flowers on my doorstep. I thought it was charming to begin with, but I now think it's creepy. I'm not comfortable, Melissa.'

'They're lovely, or they were. But they're looking tireder than tired. Dead, deceased, expired, departed, no more, passed on – throw them out, lay them to rest, consign them to the earth, bury them.'

Imogen laughed and weaved her way through the narrow space between the chairs. She held out a card. 'This note was with them.'

'Peculiar. D'you think it's Mike?'

'I've no idea. I doubt if it's Mike, flowers are not his scene, nor chocolates. This box of Thornton's arrived on the doorstep this morning without a note. Have one.'

'Thanks, I will. I like these, even though they don't go with wine. Very odd. I wonder who he is.'

'Or she.'

Melissa snorted. 'That would be a new one for you.'

'I've had a couple of texts as well. This one came in this morning.' Imogen held her phone for her friend to see.

Melissa read it out '"*So pretty, so self-assured, so talented. You are the epitome of a woman who will climb to the very top. I am faithful to you.*" Weird. You're being stalked, Imo.'

'It is weird, but it's harmless. I can live with it.'

'Harmless so far. We'll have to see what happens.'

'Who would do this? Only someone from the school. I don't know anyone else from around here.'

'I want to know. Go through them.'

'There's Connor, the boss; Sonia the senior instructor; Mike, Craig, Jimmy and Cuff. I can't see any of them stalking me, even Mike, who's always trying to be in control.'

'Another student?'

'Some of them haven't even started shaving yet. Surely not. No, my money's on Mike looking for another way to control me.'

Imogen was in a café from which delicious coffee aromas that titillated one's taste buds could be detected all the way down the street. She was deliberating over what she should do about her relations with Mike, and had chosen a corner table at the back of the place where the lighting was subdued, as if it would help her to think more clearly. She glanced around to see if anybody was watching, prior to licking the chocolate off the foam on her cappuccino. Surreptitiously, she looked up to see if anyone had noticed her display of manners of which her mother would never have approved.

Cuff sat at a table near the door. He was wearing his

company uniform, but had removed the epaulettes. Was this an opportunity to meet him and see if he wanted to join her? She examined her conscience. Two-timing anyone was something she would never consider, but here she was about to do just that. Was her association with Mike so weak that meeting another man was acceptable? Better not – Melissa was due to join her in ten minutes.

Cuff tugged his sleeves up his forearms. He often did that. Was it a habit, or was he deliberately exposing the scars to invite comment? That was the sort of thing Mike would do, attract attention to himself. Give Cuff the benefit of the doubt and assume it was a habit. After all, he seemed to possess enough self-confidence not to have to seek recognition. The scars were ugly, relatively fresh and, because they were so obvious and unusual, she was curious as to what on earth had caused them.

Cuff took his phone out of his jacket pocket and began texting. He spent some time deliberating what to write before he typed rapidly. It was clear when he finished and pressed 'Send', because he gave a final flourishing push and sat back.

Seconds later her phone gonged its message tone: *'You're absolutely gorgeous.'*

Melissa appeared above her and pulled out a chair. 'Hi,' she said. 'What's the matter? You look stunned.'

Imogen showed her the text. 'It's that new instructor, Cuff Scott. He's over there near the door. He's just sent a text and a moment later one lands on my phone. It must be him stalking me.'

'How do you know it's him? He could have sent a message to anyone. Do you know his number?'

'No, but the timing was exact. When we met he looked at me in an intense, engaging way. I'm not sure how to describe it. We shook hands. He held mine too long, and his eyes locked on mine. They wouldn't let go.'

'And what did you feel then?' Melissa's grin was wide and naughty.

'A strong attraction, I admit. I thought about it for a long time afterwards, because he seemed nice; but this attention is weird. I keep catching him looking at me. He engages my eyes and holds them longer than a normal glance.'

'You're a pretty girl, Imo. That's what men do, they're attracted by pretty girls, so they like to look at us. As long as it's not invasive, it's harmless. It's all part of the mating game. What do you do when he looks at you? Do you look back at him, do you smile? Be honest, do you catch his eye sometimes?'

'Well … yes. He seems nice, and I don't want to be unpleasant. It's just that with this stalking, his approach seems suspicious. Why doesn't he say something instead of doing creepy anonymous things.'

'Maybe he's shy. Maybe he's actually gay. Maybe he has a history. The truth will out at some stage.'

'He's not shy and he's not gay. Actually, at a party the other night, right in front of Mike, he asked me to dance. I don't know whether he really wanted to dance or was deliberately provoking Mike. Mike was furious, but I thought it was very funny. Then he left with a set of twins all to himself.'

Melissa raised her eyebrows. 'Lucky man. Perhaps it was completely innocent. Perhaps all he was doing was seeing them home. Don't jump to conclusions. And in any case, it's not your business.'

'No, but if he's a womaniser, if he just wants conquests, then it's scary he's stalking me.'

'I think you should introduce me to him. Let me suss him out.'

He eased himself off the bed, ignoring the hands which

stretched out to hold him back.

'Cuff, don't leave us. We don't want you to go anywhere.'

'Bathroom. I'll be back.'

A feeling of emptiness, as if he hadn't eaten in days, and yet he wasn't hungry – just drained. Thank God he was young and could keep up.

'You two are exhausting.'

'Is it not good, Cuff? It is good for us. We are having fun.'

He clambered over Anna to lie between them – or was she Hannah? Did it matter? She grabbed him as he did so.

'No, Anna, let the poor boy rest. We need him strong for round two.'

Cuff gave a mock groan. 'Tell me, why do you insist on coming here at night? Why don't we go to a pub for a drink for a change, before we come back here?'

'It is better to drink here, then we can have sex straight away. If we go to a pub, we have to walk here and lose time and go off the boil. We bring the wine, not so?'

'You two are never off the boil. We should go to your flat sometimes.'

'It is not suitable, Cuff. We are visiting our auntie. She is German, but her husband was English. He died, but she has bad times even now. We come here to help her for a little bit, to cheer her up. We will go home soon. Until then we can have some fun with you. It helps to undo the sadness in her house, you understand?'

Cuff understood.

'I've never met any twins before, so I don't know. You two form a unit which leaves everyone else on the outside. I can't ask one of you a question, it has to be both of you. When we have sex, you act as one to share me out between you. Do all twins behave like this?'

As if to reinforce what he said, their first three words – 'Oh, Cuff, sorry' – were uttered in unison before Hannah continued: 'We don't want you to feel pushed away, but yes, we are very close and share everything. It is natural for us. You are right, we are as one. We call ourselves Black Widows, actually.'

'Widows so young, both of you – or do you kill after mating?'

They laughed. 'We have not killed you yet. No, we just like to put fear into the hearts of men.'

But why do they always come at night? Their explanation that it's after they've settled 'Auntie' for the evening is a bit thin. Do they want to avoid being seen for some reason?

Should I care? Actually, it's good that they come here after dark, because with Imogen living opposite, there'd be a chance she'd spot them in the daytime. But why should I worry what Imogen thinks? For whatever daft reason, she's Mike Penny's girlfriend, isn't she? There was, however, something about her that he could not brush away with that simple excuse.

Cuff hadn't been getting enough exercise lately, so he decided to walk to the airfield on a Thursday in July. He would not be there before his first student, whom he nicknamed Mister Keen, but there was plenty of time. As he left his building, Imogen was wheeling her bike out of the house opposite, and he was pleased to once again get a response to his wave. In spite of his current reluctance for any serious engagement with women – the twins were only a young man's fantasy come true, it would never last – it should be easy to find a chance to talk to Imogen and learn more about her, except for the fact that Mike Penny lived below him.

Mike was holding forth in the crew room when Cuff walked in. A small group of students were listening to him, including Imogen and Mr Keen. Mike was telling them about a technique for short take-offs from bush strips. 'Yah put the flaps down just before you get flying speed during take-off.

Yer little airie will jump into the air. As soon as yer clear of the ground, yah raise the flaps, reduce the drag and get a better climb.'

Cuff could not listen to this. He walked away to quell his urge to confront Mike, but hesitated and asked himself what his alter ego would do. Would 'Jonathan' remain silent?

He called Mike away from the group. 'What you're talking about is a tricky and advanced manoeuvre and not something students should even think about trying. You have to be very careful about raising the flaps or you'll fall back to the runway. The technique's only used by experienced bush pilots. There's no need for it in the sort of flying these guys are going to do.'

Mike went red. He made no attempt to keep his voice down and tapped the two bars on his epaulettes to make his point. 'What the fuck d'yer think yer doing telling me what's right or wrong? What the hell do yah know about it? I'm a bloody sight more experienced than yah are.'

The students edged closer.

'Not so much, actually. Have you ever tried that technique? It requires very careful handling, and you shouldn't be telling students how to do it, especially since you're not explaining some very important details. Anyone trying this trick without considering them will be in for an accident. Have you ever practised it?'

Mike hesitated for a moment.

'Have you ever practised it?' Cuff insisted.

'Nah, but it's simple, and anyways we was just talking.' His teeth were bared, his fists opening and closing at his sides.

'It's not simple, it requires delicate handling. And I can think of one student who's adventurous enough to go and try it on his own, and if he does he'll be doing it with inadequate instruction.' Cuff glanced across the room. Mr Keen had the grace to look embarrassed. 'Irresponsible,' he added.

Mike looked at his audience for a moment. He must have read the doubt and confusion on their faces, because he gave the door a vicious shove and strode outside, putting a cigarette between his lips.

Imogen retrieved a bottle of white wine from her fridge, while her friend Melissa kicked off her Crocs and plonked herself down on a two-place settee. She was still wearing her dark-green veterinary nurse's tunic over her black slacks. She looked good in it, and knew it, because some of her own clothes were the same colour combination.

'How's the flying going? How's old Ma What's-her-face?'

Imogen filled the glasses. A few crumbs lay on the table; she wetted her finger and dabbed them up. She handed a glass to Melissa and sat on the only other chair, an old blue wingback with little gold fleur-de-lis emblems scattered over it. It had been in a second-hand shop window, and she had snapped it up purely for its comfort – it did not match anything else in the flat. She studied her friend, as she often did. Melissa had an engaging face, not particularly pretty but striking, with a slightly pointed chin, bold cheekbones and a strong nose. Her mouth was wide and readily spread into an attractive smile. She was a good friend.

'Old Ma Mavis is actually a lovely lady,' Imogen answered. 'I'm enjoying working for her, even though it's irregular so I never know when I'm going there or for how long. She spends days thinking what she's going to write before she sends for me. I add her thoughts to her manuscript and read it all back to her, and then she changes everything. Her sight is poor. Sadly, she might be going blind, so it must be very difficult for her to compose her words and remember what they were without me there.'

She took a sip of wine. 'Mmm, that's nice. The flying's

great, actually. I'm able to get about three or four hours a week at the moment. If this rate keeps up, which depends on Mavis, I should be finished around the end of August. The only thing is, Mike says my progress is not fast enough to complete the course in the normal average of fifty-five hours, but he won't explain why he says that.'

'Is he a good instructor? You look good in that dark-red blouse, by the way. Is it new?'

'Thanks – yes. I don't have anyone to compare him with. I've been checked by Connor, but that's a check ride not an instructional flight, so he doesn't teach much.'

Imogen stood and walked over to the window. The view looked out across the street to the block of flats where Mike stayed. 'An interesting thing happened the other day …' She went on to tell her friend about the row between Mike and Cuff. 'Mike was livid. He was so embarrassed he went outside to sulk.'

'You sound disenchanted, Imo. Mind you, I've never heard you be ecstatic over him. How did you get mixed up with him anyway?'

'He was appointed as my instructor. I thought he flew pretty well, and he talks himself up quite effectively. He asked me out early on in the course. He seemed a nice guy, and one thing led to another after I got drunk on the first night. I asked him if it was okay for an instructor to have a relationship with his student, and he said this wasn't a university, and we were both over sixteen. But in the last two weeks – since the party, in fact – he's become more and more bossy. Sometimes I don't want to do what he wants me to, but I find it difficult to refuse because of the pressure he puts on me.'

Melissa took a long sip of wine. 'It sounds as if you accept what he tells you because of his position as your instructor. Your relationship was set up as master and student from the start, and you've let it stay that way. You shouldn't let his bossiness continue outside the flying environment, though. Where's this relationship going?'

Imogen shrugged her shoulders. 'Oh, nowhere.'

'Then why not stop it now and free yourself?'

'Because I'm scared of what effect it might have on my training; I don't want bad relations with him. I'm determined to fly large jets, and you know me, I'm not going to let anything stand in my way. Mike may be right, I might not be up to standard at the moment. But it's early days still, and I know I'll be good enough eventually. By hook or by crook, I'm going to get there.'

Imogen was still looking out of the window. It was raining. 'There's been a couple more texts since I last saw you – still harmless.' She pointed. 'Here comes Mike now.'

'I must be off anyway. I'll leave you to your troubles. Seriously, Imo, there's something suspicious about the anonymous gifts and texts you've had. Please be careful and keep me up to speed. If it's not kosher, we'll fight it together.'

Imogen smiled her thanks and opened the door as Mike knocked. He came in immediately without waiting for Melissa, who had to stand back to let him in.

'Hi,' he said, without looking at her.

'Hi. Bye,' she said in a monotone and walked out, her wavy blonde hair bouncing on her shoulders.

'Mike, why won't you tell me what's wrong with my flying? Why do you think I'm behind where I should be at this stage? You won't give me a direct answer. I'm almost halfway through now, and in about seven weeks I'll have the hours for my licence. I'm keen to move on with my life. I just need to get through the skills test.'

They were sitting together on Imogen's small sofa, watching some crime drama Mike had found on the TV. He had just been outside for a smoke. She wrinkled her nose at the acrid stench on him. *Why do I put up with this?*

'Baby, seven weeks is a long time. What I'm saying is that at this stage yah ain't polished. Yer coming along okay, but I reckon yer'll need a couple of extra weeks, maybe ten hours. It ain't nothing to worry about – plenty of people learn a bit slow and then accelerate to be really good. I'm making sure yah pass first time and don't cry yer eyes out for failing. I told yah already where yah make mistakes. Yah need to listen to what I say and stop repeating errors.'

'What errors? I keep asking you, but you never give me a clear answer.'

The programme ended. Mike stood and switched off the set. 'Yah know what? We should talk about this in the briefing room. Let's forget about it and go to bed early.'

'Not tonight, I'm tired.'

Mike crossed the room from the TV to her little hi-fi set. He had left a small selection of CDs in her flat. The Sex Pistols blared out of the speakers in a blast of sound that made her jump.

'Mike, turn that off! You know I hate that music, and it's far too loud.'

He grinned back at her, gyrating to the beat, then turned the volume up.

She leapt to her feet. '*Mike!*'

He slowly turned the volume down again before switching the stereo off, still smiling at his little joke.

'You should leave. I want to go to bed.'

Immediately contrite, he came up to her and hugged her, enveloped her in his arms and, burying his head in her hair, kissed her neck. 'Sorry. I was joking. Don't take it seriously. I'm crazy about yah, baby.'

This approach used to mollify her, but now she was wooden. She was going to snap at him that she was no longer interested, that she was tired of their relationship, and that he should get the hell out of her flat and not come back, but her words did not emerge like that. 'It's okay, but I do want to go to bed to sleep. Another time. Please go.'

'Okay, baby. Sorry eh?'

4

10–14 July

Imogen was bored with the look of her flat. What it needed was a move of furniture and a change of decoration – pictures and ornaments. It wasn't practical to move the TV, which was a pity, because it governed the position of the other furniture. The best she could do was to switch the chairs around. The little kitchen needed to be reorganised as well. This would require some thought, holistic thought. Lily, her old rag doll, would certainly remain in her commanding position to oversee all activities. Imogen chuckled. *I hope she's never interrogated by MI5, it would be most embarrassing!*

She would start with the second gift of flowers, which were dying. That did not require decision: to the rubbish they must go. She had discovered them, just like the first bunch, on the doorstep first thing in the morning. There had been no note.

It was as if none was necessary; the precedent had already been set, the message was the same. As she turfed them heads first into the bin, she reflected that Mike had made no comment on them at all. Did he assume they were decoration, or what? He was the type who would have challenged her out of jealousy and asked who had sent them. Or perhaps he knew very well where they came from.

Her musing strayed to yesterday lunchtime. She had taken Melissa out to the airfield, introduced her to Cuff and left them to chat while she went off to do some preparation for her afternoon flight with Mike. It was obvious her friend was impressed by Cuff. In fact she said he was dishy and sexy, and pleasant with it. He was genuine, she insisted. Melissa was a bit *too* taken with the man, and her opinion was therefore biased. Imogen's thoughts were interrupted by Mike's characteristic knock.

'Hi.'

'Hi.' He looked her up and down for a moment. 'Why are you wearing shit clothes like that?'

She frowned at this latest criticism. These episodes of disparagement were becoming more frequent. Most annoying, and unjustified in her opinion, were the remarks about her flying skills.

'I'm going to reorganise my flat. And I'll bloody well wear what I like to do the job.' It came out with more force than she meant, and she was suddenly wary of his reaction.

He ignored the last part of her answer. 'That's great. I was getting tired of it.'

The implication in his response was too much. She couldn't stop herself. 'It's none of your business, actually. If you don't like my flat you can stop coming in.'

'Whoah! Steady girl, no offence meant. I'm just talking.' He came closer and took her hands, pulling her towards him until their faces touched. He kissed her tenderly on the forehead, broke away and gazed into her eyes for a moment. She returned his searching with a complete absence of feeling. He did not react as she feared – perhaps he never noticed – and put his arms around her. His hard, muscular body had previously excited her; it was so masculine. She had enjoyed it, even if she'd never had strong feelings for him. But now, somehow, it left her cold, it was foreign. She stayed unresponsive, willing him to let her go.

'Forget the flat. I'll help yah out of those old clothes instead.' He leered at her for a moment, but broke away and went over to his jacket. 'I've got a present for yah.'

From the pocket he drew a small plastic bag and held it out. She took it, curious. He had never given her a present before. She peered inside before putting her hand in, but didn't recognise what she was seeing: something circular, some soft black material, a glint of metal. He was watching her closely. She glanced at him, a quizzical expression on her face, before pulling out a pair of padded handcuffs.

'What the hell?' Imogen shouted as she tossed them away, opening her fingers and pulling her hand back to her chest as if they had stung her. She stared at the restraints before kicking them across the room. 'You bloody creep! No bloody way are you going to use those. Forget it. That is not my scene.'

'Come on, baby. It's only a game, yer'll enjoy it. Submission'll really turn yah on. Yer'll love it.' He bent down, picked up the offensive items and spun them around in front of her. 'Give it a try?'

'In your dreams, Mike. The only way those are going to be used is on you. I'll cuff you to the bedhead. How about that?'

The smile on his face weakened. 'No, no. That ain't the way it works.'

'It's the only way it's going to work.'

Pulling out a packet of cigarettes, he slowly selected one,

put it between his lips and felt for his lighter.

She responded to his provocation by pointing. 'Outside. You don't smoke in here.'

Still looking at her, he nodded, but lit the cigarette anyway and blew a puff of smoke into the room as he opened the door.

Imogen clenched her fists and crossed her arms. To hell with the consequences to her flying.

Minutes later Mike came back blowing his final exhalation into the room.

'Mike, I've had enough. Our relationship ends right now.'

He went so puce he looked about to explode.

A minute's silence.

He pointed a shaking finger at her. 'Yer've got the hots for Scott, haven't yah? Forget it, he's an inexperienced nothing. He's also got a dodgy past – death and divorce. Do yahself a favour and look him up on Google. I'll make it easy for yah: put in "Cuthbert Jonathan Scott inquest". I'll check back to find out what yah think.'

'I saw you the other night. You did not look happy. You're so lovely in every possible way. It's not right for such a beautiful person to be unhappy.'

Imogen put her phone away. This was weird: two lots of flowers, chocolates and a romantic text almost every day – where was this leading? She gave a mental shrug; it was harmless enough, if a bit annoying. Although this one could mean she was being watched, which was not a comfortable feeling at all. Extra vigilance and more notice of the people around her was required. Try to see if anyone was following her; see people's reactions and the attention they paid her, even the friendly crowd at the school – especially them.

Connor's door was closed, but he was visible through the

window. Imogen watched for a few seconds while he shuffled through the papers on his desk as if he was looking for something. She knocked. He peered over the top of his glasses and beckoned her in.

'Imogen. What can I do for you?' That hint of arrogance in his humourless face – was it there when he addressed all students, or was it reserved for her?

'I want a change of instructor if you can, please.'

His eyebrows went up, his tone aggressive, as usual. 'Really, why?'

Connor always made her nervous for no identifiable reason. He was more offhand with her than anyone else, but maybe it was simply in contrast to the attention most people gave her. 'Well, Mike and I have been, er, going out for a while …'

'So I heard. Bit silly in my opinion. Would never have been allowed in the Air Force. Bound to lead to trouble. In civil life I can do nothing about it, of course. What's happened?'

'I've ended the relationship. I can't continue to fly with him; plus he's very critical, whereas I don't think I'm as bad as he says.'

'Who's the instructor, you or him?'

'He is, of course. Look, I don't want to complain about him or get him into trouble. It's just that I feel I would progress better with someone else.'

'Hmm.' He looked up at a board on the wall which showed all the staff, their experience and when their training, licences and medicals were due, as well as which students they had. 'The only person with capacity for another student is Cuff Scott. He's a good pilot, but not an experienced instructor. You can go to him. I'll be here to keep a close watch on your progress.'

'Oh. Um … Is there no one else?'

'What's the matter? Is there something personal about that

option as well? I'm afraid you can't pick and choose. The school is one student short of full capacity; to give you Sonia or one of the others would disrupt the training of other students as I would have to shuffle everyone around. It wouldn't be fair on them.'

Imogen stared glumly at him. *Am I about to jump from the frying pan into the fire? If Cuff was creepy, was this a wise move?* She had nothing concrete to pin on him, only a suspicion, whereas she knew that to continue with Mike now that she had made up her mind to leave him would be awful. She needed Melissa's support and opinion. If Cuff tried to take advantage of his position, she'd have him prosecuted. Maybe she'd have to leave the school. That would bring her progress to a halt. *I'll have to brave it out.*

'Okay, Connor,' she said. 'Cuff will be fine. I'm sorry to cause you the trouble.'

'I'll brief him. He'll contact you straightaway.'

'Thanks.'

He waved a dismissive couple of fingers at her and went back to his paperwork.

Melissa ran her fingers up the back of her neck and through her thick blonde hair, tossing it up a few times and letting it cascade down her back. 'Give me wine, you meanie, then tell me your troubles. Auntie Mel will solve all – suitably lubricated, of course.'

'I've broken up with Mike.'

'Oh, thank God for that. What I can't work out is why an intelligent girl like you dithered for so long. What triggered this?'

'An accumulation of his smoking, taunting me with ghastly music, avoiding telling me why I won't pass my final skills test and, worst of all, asking me to be handcuffed to the bed!'

Melissa burst into peals of laughter. 'That's hilarious. Good on you, Imo. I'd have bloody smacked him.'

'He went away, then he came back the next day. He ranted and raved, said Connor had called him in and told him I was now Cuff's student.'

Melissa raised a single eyebrow and took a sip of wine.

'He carried on about how inexperienced Cuff was, how much of a tosser he was and how little he knew about flying. He seemed to be more angry that his nose was out of joint in Cuff's favour than that he had lost me. The thing is, it was Connor's decision, not mine.'

'You know what?' Melissa sat forward and became serious. 'I think Mike has been treating you the way he has because he likes to control you. Now that you've chucked him, he's lost that control, and the worst is he's lost it to the man who embarrassed him, as you told me. He'll imagine Cuff will take his place in all respects. His pride is severely dented.'

'It's not going to be in all respects, I promise you. I'm sure Cuff is the creep that's sending me messages. If that's true, then maybe I've stepped into the fire. Mike wasn't dangerous, just controlling. He said I should Google Cuff: he has a bad history. I'll do it now.'

'I told you before – having met him, even if briefly, I reckon Cuff is on the level. He's a decent guy. My gut feeling, and it's seldom wrong.'

'We'll see.'

Imogen switched on her laptop while Melissa topped up their glasses.

'I still can't tell you two apart, so I'm going to call you both H-Anna.'

'It is easy to see the difference: Hannah has a birthmark, and I don't.'

'Where?'

Hannah switched on the light and showed him.

Cuff laughed. 'Very pretty, but I can't take your panties off every time I want to get your names right. You'll stay as H-Anna for me.'

'We want to know what is your best pleasure, Cuff. What is the thing you like best right now?'

'You two. And if we could be young forever, it would stay that way.'

They both giggled, and Hannah put the light off again. Her hand came back to stroke his chest, gradually getting lower. Anna's hand was on his thigh, creeping up.

'Also, Cuff, what is your worst fear? What makes you have a panic?'

'I should tell you that? You might do it to me.'

'Don't be silly. Why would we do terrible things to a man who is giving us such fun?'

'You call yourselves Black Widows, so anything is possible.'

If it had been light, he would be searching their faces for the truth, but it wasn't and their hands had almost reached their goal.

'I'm a little claustrophobic, so being shut in, or even in a lift, is very unpleasant for me. Also any kind of restraint, even if accidental … I find it very disturbing.'

'Oh, yes, we don't like that also.'

Mentally, Cuff swore at himself. Why had he admitted to those weaknesses? Stupid. But they had given him no reason not to trust them, and they would be gone soon, home to Germany.

Cuff had taken his car to the airfield for once, because he wanted to go into town afterwards to stock up on food. He drove away after flying with Mister Not-So-Keen, who spent most of his hour's instruction revising what he had learned ten days ago instead of moving on to the next exercise.

On the way back to his flat, he stopped at some traffic lights, which were set to give priority to the main road and a turning lane, and so took a long time to change. He applied his parking brake and sat back to wait, idly watching the activity at a hand car wash across the road.

The place was staffed by men, who all appeared similar – black-haired and dark-eyed. They moved rapidly around the vehicle they were washing, yellow buckets to hand and cloths being wielded with great energy. Soapsuds streamed off the car in white rivulets, leaving bubbles to pop and die on the tarmac.

Another vehicle was parked to the side, not in the queue for a wash. The driver got out and went to the office. Cuff's interest perked up – it was Mike Penny. As Mike approached the door, a tough-looking character came out. He shouted something at the washers before turning to Mike. The two conversed for a while before the man gripped Mike's sleeve and pulled him into the office. The lights changed without Cuff noticing, and he jumped as someone hooted at him.

Cuff was waiting at the coffee machine for Sonia to finish when Connor strode through the crew room, muttering angrily to himself and clutching his phone. Without any form of greeting, he called out, 'Sonia!' and inclined his head towards his office.

'Sorry, Cuff, I'd better get one for him as well.'

Cuff stood back. 'No problem, go ahead.'

He knew Sonia's normal routine was to run to work, then change into her uniform. There were no showers, but that was not something which appeared to worry her. Still in her tracksuit, she carried both cups through to Connor's office and closed the door.

She came out a few minutes later, by which time Craig and

Jimmy had joined Cuff.

'What's up, Sonia? I hear alarm bells.' Jimmy inclined his head towards Connor.

'Mike has had an accident and sprained or broken his ankle or something.' She mopped at a bead of sweat below her right ear with a little towel she kept tucked into her waist band. 'Apparently his leg's in a cast, and he won't be able to fly for a while. He'll be in later. We'll find out then how long he's going to be out of it. Connor's going to reallocate his students, which means we'll all get an extra one. The plus side is Mike will have to take over some of the lecture slots.'

'Bang goes my afternoon nap,' said Craig.

Sonia was more serious. 'I don't need this right now. My mother's moving into a care home, and there's a lot of extra work attached to that for a while.'

Imogen made no effort to go and help Mike struggle with the self-closing door and a pair of crutches while hopping on his good right leg. Three students rushed over, though. He grinned at them and shrugged them off, managing on his own. He was wearing navy shorts with his medical boot, and a red golf shirt. The whole performance was overacted.

'What happened, Mike?'

'Is it bad?'

'Does it hurt?'

And the obviously stupid question: 'Can you still fly?'

'Nah,' he answered, 'not for a month, the doctor says. It's a grade-two or moderate sprain, and I've gotta wear this boot. But I'm pretty fit so it should heal quicker. It's important to take care of it to save problems in the future.'

Imogen gave a snort of derision, turned her back and broke away from the group. She lacked the patience to witness this pathetic, attention-seeking performance. The conversation still followed her to the far side of the room, though.

'What happened, Mike? How did you do it?'

'I saw this guy going to mug a little old lady last night. I ran and tackled him, but in the fight I slipped off the kerb and, 'bang', my ankle went. Bastard got away, but at least the old lady was okay.'

'Wow!'

'Fantastic! Great, Mike.'

'Our local hero!'

'Nah. Any one of yah would have done the same thing, but thanks, guys. I'd better go and speak to the boss.' He hobbled away, knocking into the prized chair en route.

Mike came back into the crew room after a few minutes.

'Imo, hi. Will yah run me to work when you're coming in? Taxis are gonna cost a bloody fortune until this boot's off.'

He had spoken loud enough for everyone to hear. To say no in front of them all was too difficult. She gave a grudging yes and clenched her teeth, angry he had succeeded in getting her back under a measure of his control.

Cuff was beside her. She stepped away, very unsure about him.

'You make your feelings obvious, I'm afraid.' He grinned at her. 'Don't worry, I'll run him in, save you the trouble, and it'll piss him off.'

'Maybe. We'll see,' she said curtly, unable to bring herself to be pleasant. What was it with these men? Mike was impossible, rude and controlling, and Cuff certainly couldn't be trusted after what she'd read about him. He had the qualities to be the stalker.

She's so beautiful to me, so alluring. She must feel my overwhelming presence and know I am her saviour. I want her to see me as a devoted lover. Someone who will support her no matter what the world throws at her. I search for signs that she is accepting me, looking forward to my messages of love, one day to welcome me in person, rushing into my arms for everlasting shelter. She doesn't know it now, but she will. Soon she will answer my messages.

I haven't contacted her since Friday. Has she longed for my words of adoration? I've missed her and must tell her so.

Imogen had just closed her front door when the house phone rang. She prayed it wasn't Mike.

Without putting down her shopping bag, she caught the call on the fourth ring. 'Hello?'

A cheery voice said, 'Hi, I'm George from the Telephone Protection Service. I'm calling to tell you we have a special offer on security on your phone. First, I need to confirm I'm talking to the correct person, the person who registered with this service. So if you can give me your full name please?'

'Imogen Greening. But I don't remember registering with you.'

'And your full address and postcode, please?'

'Look, I think you have this wrong. I have never registered with any telephone service.'

'My records show that a Ms Imogen Greening is registered. Now if I could just have your full address and post code, please?'

'If you have this phone number, then you will know the address, surely.'

The caller hung up.

Was that him? There's a scam that starts the same way and ends up asking for your credit card details. Maybe he was pretending to be a scammer: deliberately botching a scam in order to scare me. He's got me on edge all right, but I'm not scared – not yet. On the contrary, I'm getting more and more angry.

5

12–16 July

Craig had organised another party. The twins said they couldn't go. Cuff was not sorry about that. Although he didn't see them every night, the frequency was enough to keep him tired and in need of some uninterrupted sleep. So much so that although there were young women there who were becoming increasingly gorgeous as the night progressed, he ignored any opportunities and drank too much. He got home somewhere around midnight on Saturday morning. As he struggled to fit the wrong key to his lock, the sound of a light aircraft passing overhead surprised him, but as he was not capable of concentrating on anything other than an urgent need to pee and crash into bed, he took no further notice.

Six hours later, his phone rang. The harsh sound pierced

his hangover, spurring him to answer it before his head burst. He rolled over and, with his eyes only half open, scrabbled around for the mobile. It was somewhere on the bedside table. He knocked it to the floor and had to lean right over to get it. He swore with the sudden pressure on his brain and the effort involved.

'Hello, Lisa.'

'Oh, Cuff, please, I need help. There's so much going wrong in this house, and I can't fix it all.'

Is there a boxer in my head? Every beat of my pulse is trying to punch its way out of my skull. Bloody hell, Lisa, it's not my bloody problem! 'What problems?'

'Well it's nothing much, they're all little things. But I can't do it all, I don't know how.'

Cuff rolled over onto his back and pulled the blankets up to his chin. 'Can't you get someone in to fix them? What's wrong, anyway?'

'They're all little things,' she repeated.

'All right, I'll take time off work and come over. Is there anything that's going to take a long time?'

'No.'

From her small voice, he knew she was lying.

He cleared two days off with Connor and made his apologies to Imogen and the other two students. Mr Keen was disappointed, and Mr Not-So-Keen couldn't have cared less. Oddly enough, with her drive to progress rapidly, Imogen should have shown some frustration, but she didn't. She passed no comment and even appeared relieved.

The baby was ten months old and crawling everywhere at high speed.

'He's a boy, and his name's Barry,' Lisa announced proudly when Cuff first arrived.

'Gawd,' he muttered under his breath. *How's the poor little bastard going to turn out with Castle's violent genes and Lisa's erratic personality?*

The child cried often while Cuff was there. Most likely it was because of Lisa's fragile emotions, but it might have been him who made it howl, as if it knew he was the man who had released his father into the void.

And was it because he had been around the screaming brat so much that Barry Castle's ghastly, panicked face woke him in the middle of the night and robbed him of sleep? Normally handsome, in fear his eyes had been wide and bloodshot, the teeth bared back to the gums, spittle spraying as he shrieked sounds of agony yet to be felt, piercing cries which echoed off the cliffs and were carried away in the chilling wind. Cuff asked himself for the umpteenth time if he could have done more to save the man who had come to kill him, but again found no answer.

Back in his flat on the Tuesday night at some ungodly hour, an odd sound dragged Cuff from his sleep. It was a soft noise, the sound of an aircraft passing overhead with the engine throttled back as if it were landing. He crossed to the window and looked up – nothing there. Its landing light came on immediately before it disappeared behind the house opposite. Because it was heading away from him, the beam was only visible as a glow reflected back from the atmosphere.

'Why is he flying with no navigation lights?' Cuff asked his empty bedroom. There should have been a white tail light heading away from him. Then he remembered he'd heard the same sound on Saturday morning. His alarm clock said it was ten to twelve, leaving some six hours to get more rest.

He tried to fall asleep. He tried too hard, gave up, climbed out of bed and studied until it was time to go out to the airfield. He had an early flight booked with Mr Keen, who had asked to be fitted in before the day's normal start time because he had something important to do. Cuff had forgotten what that something was; it didn't matter, he enjoyed the early morning and this was a beautiful one, clear with a light breeze. After Mr Keen was his first flight with Imogen.

He reached the airfield long before his student, checked the aircraft's technical documents and walked out to the parking area. After his accident four years previously, he carried out his preflight inspections with extreme diligence. On that occasion he, as a more youthful student, had missed the flash grenade which had been taped to his fuel line and led to his crash. That was not likely to happen again, but Cuff made sure he never missed anything which was out of place or looked as if it might fail.

He opened the front cowling. The engine was warm. *What the hell's going on? It's not hot, but it's nowhere near as cold as it should be after a night out in the open. That aircraft landing without lights; it was this one.* He went back to the office to review the documentation. There was no record of the aeroplane having flown either last night or on Saturday, and the hours recorded at the end of yesterday's flight matched the Hobbs meter, an instrument in the cockpit which records the flying hours.

Even if the aircraft had not flown, the engine had certainly been on a few hours before, but why? *Who has run this engine? Who is flying without navigation lights at midnight?*

For further confirmation, he checked the fuel gauge. It showed a fraction short of the F mark. Cuff climbed up on the wing and opened the fuel cap. Sure enough, the level was just below normal. This was not impossible, but unlikely, as the instructors were pretty good at seeing that the aeroplanes were always topped up after their last flight of the day. He was still trying to work out the possibilities when Mr Keen arrived and the day began.

He found it difficult to concentrate at first. Mr Keen's chirpiness was irritating, and for Cuff to respond cheerfully was difficult. Those two days of Lisa had soured his normal buoyant mood as well. And the night flights – they were a puzzle. Someone was doing something illegal. Why? What?

Craig and Jimmy were always super-friendly towards Imogen. Whenever either of them had nothing else to do they would seek her out and chat her up. As a pretty girl, she had come to accept this approach. In fact, in small doses she enjoyed the banter – they were harmless guys, after all. Cuff, on the other hand, was more serious and an enigma. The way he looked at her and his easy smile were clear signs he was attracted to her, so why wasn't he more forthcoming? Because of Mike, or simply out of respect for the status quo?

That was how she used to think, but, as she had pointed out to Melissa: 'He's divorced after just over a year, during which time he had an affair, staged his own disappearance, and either pushed a man over the cliff or let him fall. He also picks up a set of twins for the night. So far, his texts have been harmless and he's been pleasant. But now I know I've got a possible murderer and a womaniser stalking me, how can I trust him? And he's now my instructor!'

'What are you going to do?'

'I can't go back to Mike. Connor won't give me to someone else, so if I want to continue flying here, then I'll have to accept Cuff. It's going to be bloody difficult working together, knowing what I know, but I'm determined to finish this course, so I'll do it. He'd better not step out of line, though.'

Imogen reached the airfield well before her first flight with Cuff. She spent the spare time pacing the crew room, and even passed up an offer of coffee. Could she go through with this? What was she going to do if he tried to take advantage of her? To respond in kind to his normal pleasant and cheerful approach would be impossible, so she was relieved when he greeted her curtly and ushered her into a briefing room.

He glanced at his watch, then at her. 'Why are you learning to fly? Pleasure? What do you expect your licence to do for you?'

'I'm going to qualify for an airline and fly big jets.'

It was a statement of fact. There was no possibility of mistaking her intentions.

Cuff gave a brief nod in response. 'We're on the same track. I'm just a little further along the road than you are.' And that was the end of any conversation unrelated to the flight. *Thank God. The last thing I want is personal talk.*

'Our first session will be more a revision than an introduction to something new. I want an overall impression of how you handle the aircraft before we progress,' he told her.

During the flight he said very little, bar asking her to perform various manoeuvres, but he appeared to enjoy it, because his mood improved significantly. It made her wary, but her need to hear his verdict on her flying overrode her concerns.

'Imogen,' he said afterwards in the briefing room, 'please understand that my comments come from a very inexperienced instructor. You are the most advanced pupil I've had, so I have no one to compare you with. Overall impression: you fly accurately and well. You're in control all the time. You appreciate what the aircraft is doing and correct accordingly. There's still quite a bit more to be learned before you can take your skills test, but I'm sure we'll get there in record time. Remember, this is my inexperienced opinion, and Connor or Sonia may think differently.'

Imogen forgot her reservations for a moment. For the first time her instructor had given her a genuine compliment.

Mike's comments had been flummery, a meaningless waste of words.

'I have one overriding observation, though. Although you fly accurately, the experience for your passenger is not comfortable. You throw the aircraft around with sudden and sometimes harsh movements of the controls. Do you ride?' He pulled his sleeves up a little.

'Yes, we have two horses at home.' Her attention was caught by a glimpse of those ugly scars on his forearms, and she determined to find out what they were. It seemed to her they were a clue to his past.

'Do you kick it hard to make it move? Do you yank its head round to turn?' He flung his arm out to the side. 'I'll bet not.'

'No, of course not.'

'Well, you should treat your little aeroplane in the same way. Show it some mechanical sympathy. Ease it into the turn, use the throttle smoothly, don't jerk it. Don't throw it around: pressure your machine into doing what you want, just as you gently nudge your horse. Apart from making for a more comfortable flight, mechanical things don't respond well to harsh treatment, even if they are unfeeling.'

What he was saying resonated with her and was completely different to Mike's coarse instruction to be 'positive' in her movements.

On the other hand, Mike was not a murdering divorcee.

Imogen had everything sorted: her flat was organised, her flight bag with her headset, maps, phone and a salad for lunch was ready to go. Why was it then, that something unusual cropped up to delay her? It seemed to happen often these days, for no apparent reason. To such an organised person, the occurrences were an irritation. Sometimes they made her grumpy for a short while; on other occasions they had no effect. Today the iron had leaked over the floor and soaked the carpet. A new iron was required, an expense that made this a grumpy day. On top of that, the last thing she wanted to do was give Mike a lift to the airfield. She hadn't had the heart to say no or refer him to Cuff, and cursed her own weakness.

A large brown envelope was lying on the mat. It was as stiff as weak card. In spite of the passing time, she was curious, slit it open, slid out the contents and gasped. Her lips tightened into a thin line, and she trembled. The moment passed. She put the envelope in a drawer out of sight and went out, slamming the front door behind her.

It was cloudy and cool outside, which did nothing to improve her mood. Mike put his crutches in first, from the footwell to the inner side of his seat, before sitting sideways and bringing his gammy leg in last. He settled in, fastened his seat belt and grinned at her. 'All set, let's go.'

She didn't answer.

'What's up with you? Yah pissed off this morning?'

She didn't answer, so he tried another tack. 'How's it going with Scott?'

'Fine.'

'What's that mean?'

Imogen didn't want to talk, and she certainly didn't feel like talking to Mike. To put him off, she replied, 'He's been away. We've only flown once.'

'A few more flights and yer'll see his weaknesses. He's not a pilot's arse. Yah can take me into town later, I need to get some stuff. It won't take long, specially if yah help carry.'

Her hackles rose, but she withheld a retort. At the airfield she left the car and walked away, leaving Mike to get out on his own. In the crew room she found Cuff talking to Jimmy and Craig. She pushed between the men and glared at Cuff. 'I'm not feeling up to flying today. I'm going home.'

'Oh, that's too bad. It's no problem, though. Is there anything I can do to help?'

'No.' She barged out of the door ahead of Mike, letting it close and leaving him to negotiate it on his own. She ignored his audible: 'Bloody bitch.'

Melissa arrived at Imogen's flat as soon as she could, which was during her lunch break.

Imogen handed her the envelope. Her fingers trembled as she held it out. But there was anger in her voice. 'Look what arrived on my mat this morning.'

Melissa glanced at her friend with concern before she opened the envelope. 'Bloody hell, Imo! This is getting serious.'

'I know when those were taken. It was at the full moon in June. It was a beautiful night, clear and as bright as anything. I stood naked in the moonlight, just back from the window, enjoying the freedom of it.'

'These are high-quality pictures. They must have been taken from directly opposite with a long lens.'

'Right, and who stays directly opposite?'

'I don't know.'

'Cuff does. That's his flat right there, same level as mine.' She pointed at the top floor of the block opposite, which, because it was set much lower than the house she lived in, was in line with her first-floor apartment.

'You must go to the police, Imo. I'll come with you.'

'No. The police don't take these things seriously. There are too many stories of women not being believed over stalking, assault, even domestic abuse. This has been a shock. I admit it's scared me. I've not reacted well so far today, but I'll pull myself together and go after this bastard on my own. I'm going to let it continue and gather as much evidence as I can to be sure I'm believed, then I'll hang him out to dry in front of the public and show the world what a bloody pervert he is. Do you realise I've been getting four or five texts a week? They're all harmless and complimentary, but it's too much. It's creepy.'

'Imo, calm down. Two things: we need to keep a close eye on his words and actions. If it starts to look threatening, we mustn't hang around, we've got to report it before any harm's done. Secondly, you had better be bloody sure it's Cuff before you accuse the wrong man.'

'Who else can it be?' Imogen snapped, and pointed, her finger quivering. 'His flat's right there. Even if it isn't him, it's got to be someone at the club. How else would he know where I live and what my number is?'

'I don't know, but as I told you before, he strikes me as being a perfectly normal, decent guy. I wouldn't rush into accusing him without concrete proof. If it's not him, then you'll wreck his life by making this public.'

'Melissa, this is getting to me. It'll eventually affect my flying, because I won't be able to concentrate. I'm determined to complete this course in the minimum time allowed. I don't want it extending because I'm shit scared of my instructor.'

'I still think we should go to the police. I hear you about gathering evidence, but leave this too long and he'll get closer and closer, and might do you some actual harm.'

I've sent so many messages of love she can be in no doubt of my feelings, but she hasn't responded. She could have replied to those messages, at least to say thank you for the compliments, but nothing. She'll be pleased with the photos – who wouldn't be – but she'll be worried, too. Oh, and those were so good. I was so lucky to see her parading her body in the moonlight. It was a positive sign for me. She's shown she's a sensual girl. Soon I will appeal to her carnal instincts. I want her to feel the need I have and titillate her with suggestive words. She needs to know my love is real.

6

16 July

The unrecorded night flights puzzled Cuff. Should he tell Connor? But what if it was Connor himself who was up to something? It would be best to find out what was going on first, which meant being there when the aircraft got home, which so far had been at a similar time each night.

So he went to bed early and set his alarm for eleven thirty. He took a while to go to sleep, wondering what risk he was exposing himself to if Connor was the pilot. Would the man fire him if he said anything? *No, hang on. That's Dad talking. I said I was going to be more like my alter ego. Would 'Jonathan' worry what Connor thought?*

By ten to twelve, Cuff had left his car in the wide entrance to a field and walked the rest of the way to the airfield. He passed the flying school, a low, dark shadow of a building under the moon, which was almost full. A set of headlights approached along the road. The beams swept over the offices and glinted on the red tail light of a vehicle parked there. That was odd – everyone should be tucked up in bed at this time of night. The car was in Connor's allocated bay, but was it his? It was. So it must be Connor who was flying.

Cuff had a quick walk around the building to confirm there was no one inside, then made his way to the parking area. Sure enough, the Cessna 172 was missing. He found himself a position which overlooked the apron and from where he could also see the runway threshold.

A little after twelve, the faint sounds of an engine came to him. Without its red, green and white navigation lights, the aeroplane was hidden in the dark until a brief shadow passed close to the moon with a whisper of wind over its wings and a murmur from its idling motor. Cuff imagined the path the pilot was taking to line up with the runway, and waited.

The sky over the approach path was empty, and the invisible aircraft was barely audible. Suddenly, a brilliant light stabbed out of the darkness aiming directly at the threshold.

'Whew! He left that to the last moment.'

There was a faint squeal as the tyres hit the tarmac. The landing light was extinguished immediately, and the Cessna rolled to a stop. The little aircraft was white, its features discernible in the moonlight.

It stayed at the runway's end for about two minutes. There was movement on the far side: three or four figures. Were they passengers? Were they unloading something? They ran, a small tight group crouching low, towards the bushes beyond the runway's edge.

Cuff retreated to behind another aeroplane and waited. The Cessna taxied slowly into the area using minimal power and parked in its normal position. A few moments later the pilot got out, opened the engine cowling and did something – his body hid his actions. He chocked the wheels before striding to the side of the hangar where he picked up two jerry cans and carried them back to the machine. Another trip back to the building, and he collected a short stepladder and a third can.

It was not possible to see who it was – he was wearing a dark hoodie and could have been from the school or outside. Connor moved with a spring in his step, as this man did. Was it him, or any other athletic person? There was no way of telling. Standing on the ladder, the pilot opened the fuel cap on top of the left wing and, using a funnel, poured most of the two jerry cans into the tank. The man took everything round to the right wing and emptied the remaining fuel into that tank. He secured the tank filler cap, collected his cans and the ladder, and took them round the front of the hangar, presumably to put them away.

There was no more to be seen from where Cuff was standing. The best thing to do was to leave before Connor – if it was him – bumped into him as he returned to the office for his car.

Sixty litres of fuel; over thirteen gallons. That's enough for an hour and a half's flying. What has he been doing? And where has Connor been?

The swans which patrolled the river where The Gargoyle's pub deck reached out over the water never seemed to be put off by the lack of human generosity. Beautiful and vain, they traded looks for food, maintaining station in the current with gentle unseen paddles. Unmoved by them, Ginny and Martin listened to Cuff's suspicions.

'Martin, I have to find out what's going on and identify this pilot. He's using an aircraft that's not his and not recording the flying time, which is both illegal and dangerous in the long term. What he's up to must be criminal, otherwise why is he cooking the books?'

Martin sniffed, his eyes lighting up; here was another chance for excitement.

Ginny, as usual, became wary and 'that look', as Martin called it, was written all over her face. Cuff grinned evilly at her. 'Don't fret Ginny, this is not dangerous. We're only going to watch what's going on, not get involved.'

Ginny cocked her ginger head to one side and gave Cuff a plain 'I don't believe you' look. 'I should never have told you to be a "Jonathan". You're reverting to type, and I see another disaster coming. You've done some very dangerous things in the past and most of them have involved Martin. He's only too willing to help – stupid man – desperate for some excitement in his life.'

'Ginny, stop looking at me like that. I've stumbled on a situation where a pilot may be stealing an aeroplane and either smuggling something, probably drugs, or trafficking migrants, or both. On one side he's dishonest and being reckless with the safety of the aircraft, and on the other, if the people I saw were passengers, who knows what's happening to them? They might be terrorists, they might end up as forced labour – slaves – and if there are women, I don't have to spell out to you what will happen to them. We have to do something about it, and we have to do it over the few days surrounding the full moon. He's using its light to see the runway, only putting on his landing light at the very last moment. The moon is full on Friday, but unfortunately the weather forecast is not good for the rest of the week so the opportunity for this month may have passed.'

'Go to the police.'

'I will, I promise, as soon as we know what's going on. It is possible there's a reasonable explanation, although admittedly I can't see what. Look, all we're going to do is watch. If there's obviously something wrong, then we can alert the police. There's no harm in that, is there?'

Ginny pursed her lips; a stern teacher to naughty boys. 'I want to know every detail. Don't try to fool me, you know I'll spot it.'

Martin gave her a hug. 'Thanks, love. We'll be good. This is the right thing to do.'

Her expression was not softened by Martin's charm. 'If this is smuggling or trafficking, we'll be dealing with some very dangerous and violent people.' She looked Cuff in the eye. 'And you, forget my advice, stop trying to be a "Jonathan".'

Imogen had never bothered to close the curtains before, except to shut out the street light. She was always sufficiently far back from the window when she walked from the bathroom to the bedroom to not be seen from the outside. She closed them now, though.

The photos of her naked had shaken her more than she thought was possible, since she was normally strong enough to brush off embarrassing things. The pictures were in black and white, their quality coming from the lightness of the high points, her breasts, belly, thighs and buttocks, curves accentuated by the shadows which followed the smooth outline of her body.

These are excellent pictures, and they do me a great deal of justice. But I did not give anyone permission to take them. He's spying on me, he's invading my life. With every text it gets worse and more sinister, even if the messages have been harmless so far. The sheer volume of it all is alarming in itself, but these photos have added a sinister dimension. I'm now pissed off, Cuff. I'm going to expose you for what you are. I'm going to have you prosecuted.

She had showered and put on her underwear when something drew her to look out of the window. The sun had already set, the daylight was fading, the cloud was lower and the evening's indistinct shadows would soon be overcome by the darkness. The street lamps' orange glare took over, each light penetrating the shadows of its neighbour and leaving few corners indistinct.

Imogen carefully drew an edge of the curtain back. Was Cuff watching from the windows of his unlit flat? He might be there in the darkness, hoping to get another glimpse of her, but there was no sign of him.

She gasped, took a step back and narrowed the gap in her curtain so only her right eye could see out. Down in the street, at the base of the lamp on the opposite side, disguised partly by the pole, stood a man.

A wide-brimmed hat ensured his face was in shadow, but there was no doubt he was looking directly at her. His eyes – invisible – were fixed on hers. They held her; she could not pull away. They penetrated her personal space. Suddenly the tiny gap in her curtain was a foot wide. He could have been right opposite her, standing there, in the flat. She shuddered and lowered the curtain carefully, hoping he would not see the movement. She stepped back from the window, took a deep breath and leaned on the table to regain her wits. Was that Cuff? Admittedly, she was not one hundred per cent sure. She had been looking down on him. It was hard to tell his height and build with the hat and the long coat, but it certainly could have been him.

This campaign of his has taken a dramatic shift from harmless texts to physical presence. 'Campaign' sounds so military, but from his perspective maybe campaign is exactly the right word for it.

Back in her bedroom she finished dressing, taking her time and calming herself. The pub where she was meeting Melissa was an easy walk down the avenue for three short blocks, then a block off to the right along the side of a small park. Not far, but the man's presence outside was unnerving, even though there were plenty of people about. *Should I phone*

Melissa and get her to come to the flat first? No. This pervert will think he's won if I hide away.

She was ready. One last look outside: the man had gone. Leaving her front door open, she walked out to the pavement and looked up and down the street. There was no sign of him. She returned to the door and closed it.

Many people were walking home from the station or the bus stop after work. *Plenty of protection for me, but plenty of cover for someone tracking me.*

The sharp rhythmic tap of hard heels struck the pavement behind her. An isolated sound amongst the soft shoes most people wore. The inclination to turn and look was strong, but it was essential to act normal. She paused at the first side street. Behind her the clicking heels slowed their rhythm. She checked for traffic and walked on. The clicking picked up pace with her. There was a block and a half to go before she would turn right. If he turned with her onto the less populated street, she'd be concerned. On this road there were so many people about, it would be impossible to confirm someone was following her.

When she reached the street she wanted, the one which ran beside the park, she took the opportunity to look back. A man in a broad-brimmed hat was thirty yards behind her and making no attempt to hide his presence.

Imogen clenched her teeth and told herself to get a grip. *I am not going to be cowed by this creep. Just let him try something and I'll, I'll …*

She crossed the main road and took the side street. It was darker, there being no lights to illuminate the pavement, only the occasional lamp over a front door and two street lights on the park side of the road. One block to go and the pub was on the corner. The clicking followed her; it echoed off the houses. What do spies do when they're followed? Stop and look back while tying your shoelaces – she had no laces. Look in a shop window and back up the street behind you – there were no shops, just a row of expensive Georgian terraced houses.

The footsteps maintained pace with her, but did not get any closer. The pub was now only a hundred yards away, its lights a cheery splash of colour. She was safe now; she could outrun him from here. At the door she turned and stared at her pursuer. He had stopped and was watching her, a deliberately sinister silhouette of a figure in a long, open coat and wide hat. A scarf covered his nose and mouth. Above it, from the shadow of the hat, his eyes again met and held hers. They caused a single shiver in her, but she determined not to be the first to blink. He turned away and crossed the road.

After a cottage pie and wine, Melissa walked back with Imogen to her flat, then ordered a taxi home. When she'd left, Imogen twice checked that the door was locked and made sure the windows were secure. She peeked round the curtain again when the lights were out, but he wasn't there. Slowly she unwound, helped by a final small whisky, and eventually fell asleep.

Melissa had said she'd call in the morning to check how she was. The house phone rang and Imogen answered with a cheery, 'Hi.'

Silence.

'Hello?'

Silence. No – a faint sound of breathing.

She slammed the receiver down.

She's nervous of him. I saw it when she looked out of her window and her eyes engaged his. She hid away. I saw it in her walk, her nervous steps, her glances back at him. She only had the courage to stare him down when she was safely at the pub.

I have been very clever. This man will prove useful. His sinister approach is working for me. Soon she'll look to me, her admirer and lover, for protection, for only I can keep her safe.

'Cuff, you are right, we should do something different for a change. Let us have a picnic in the woods.'

'Great idea. I'm free on Friday afternoon and the weather should be okay – it may be cloudy, but it shouldn't rain.'

'Okay. We will organise. We will make a German *picknick* for you. So sad; it will be the last time we meet; we go home the day after. We found a very private spot.'

Anna giggled. 'No one will see us. We want you to remember us for the rest of your life.'

7

18–21 July

Craig was inclined to use his height to his advantage. He had a manner of leaning over people so they had to stretch their necks to meet his deep blue eyes, which was especially difficult for the shorter ones. Imogen was sure he didn't do it intentionally: he wasn't the kind of person who enjoyed making people uncomfortable, especially girls. He put his hand up on the wall above her head to support his forward lean and gazed down on her with an adoring look. 'Imogen, I would really like to take you out for a slap-up meal. We'll have a fun evening, lots to talk about.'

Imogen put a hand on his chest to push him back and regain her personal space. 'Craig, I think we could have a nice evening, but—'

'Great, how about—'

'But,' she insisted, 'I'm not available, I'm not going to have a one-to-one anything with anyone from the school.'

'Aww.'

'Craig, you're a super guy. I mean that, but no. Not you, nor anyone round here.'

'You're such a treasure, Imogen. For you, I'll leave the school and then we can go out.' He was grinning, showing all his large teeth. 'I'll not stop trying, you know.'

She laughed, patted his arm and went to get a cup of coffee.

'Imo.' Mike left his crutches leaning against the wall and hopped across the crew room to her, using the chairs for additional support. 'I've got an idea that'll really help: yah can lend me yer car. It's automatic so I won't have to use my left leg to drive, and I can save on taxis.'

I don't believe he asked me that. 'No. The car is not insured for you, and if I were to add you to the insurance I would have to guarantee your fitness to drive. If I lie about that and you have an accident, my insurance will crucify me, let alone not pay any claim.'

'Yah don't use the car much, and all I'll do is go from here to my flat and back. I thought, since yah won't give me a lift every day, yah could help.'

'That's only one reason why I won't let you drive the car, but I'm not going to hide behind my insurance. Even if they did allow it, I wouldn't lend it to you.'

'Well, at least yah could run me around a bit. Help more with my shopping and stuff.'

His mocking grin was deliberate and detestable. Imogen stalked off without answering. *He knows he'll never get me to lend the car, he just wants to rile me. And I'm so bloody stupid in reacting exactly as he wants. He didn't even ask, he made a suggestion and didn't even have the decency to say please. What a difference between him and Craig. Mike is an absolute prick.*

* * *

Imogen opened the door to the pub, but glanced back along the street before going in. He was standing there again, watching her. She marched over to Melissa's table and slid onto a bench seat. 'I'm now bloody furious. I'm sick to death of this man. I'm going to turn his bloody balls into a bolas!'

Melissa giggled. 'That's my girl. What are you going to catch with your bolas, always assuming they've got enough weight, of course?'

'Ha, ha. Actually, bad idea. You've got a point. This creature's balls more than likely have no weight at all. Seriously, Melissa, Cuff followed me again tonight, still wearing his absurd bloody hat. I stopped a couple of times and turned round. Each time he was just standing there, about thirty or forty yards away and doing nothing. Last time, I'd had enough. I went towards him. I don't know what I was going to do, I don't know what I would have done if he'd stood his ground. But he didn't, he walked away, and I only saw him again just before I came in here.'

'Imo, be cross, but don't be stupid. If you're going to challenge the man directly, you could get hurt. Please. So you still think it's Cuff?'

Imogen threw her hands in the air. 'Even God doesn't know what I think any more. In the school environment he's professional, kind and patient; he gives me no reason to feel threatened. But everything points to him, all the things we've already discussed stack up against him. He's more likeable than Mike, and he's certainly a better instructor than Mike. How can he be so different from one moment to the next? Is it possible for a nice person to be so perverted?'

A bout of raucous laughter erupted at the bar, drowning out her words. One man was in hysterics, and his beer slopped to the floor before he put the mug down.

'What? Say that again.'

'I said, I'm trying to separate my thoughts into two streams. One with my flying and the instructor who is getting the best out of me, and the other this stalking thing. These two must not meet. That way I can have the right relationship with Cuff, focus on achieving my goal to finish top of the class, so to speak, and not be bothered by the stalker until I leave the school environment.'

'Great feat if you can manage it.'

'It's working so far. It's easier than I thought, probably because Cuff has not put a foot wrong, professionally speaking. He treats me as he would any other student, which gives me the confidence to carry on with him. We had a great flight this morning, and he thinks I'm progressing well. He was quite distant though – more than normal. He ignored me after the debrief. Not that I'm complaining, as I don't want to encourage him in any way. In fact, with my instructor stalking me, and Mike … I'm very much off men.'

Imogen paused and sipped her wine. One of the men at the bar was telling another joke, while the others leaned in to hear, which probably meant it was crude.

'I didn't tell you, but he was away last weekend and Monday on some personal business, so I didn't fly. During the whole time he was away, nothing happened. No texts, no one following or watching me, no gifts, nothing. But as soon as he's back, I get this.' She pulled her phone out of her pocket. '"*You are so lovely. I adore you, and I've missed you.*" If that's not an admission of who he is, I don't know what is. Then I get another text immediately after Cuff has been typing on his phone in the crew room.' She passed her phone across the table. 'I watched him do it.'

Melissa's eyes narrowed as she read out loud, '*My thoughts linger on your beautiful form. My fingers stroke your creamy skin, arousing you, soft and titillating.*' She put her hand over Imogen's. 'Take it easy, my friend, you're starting to stress too much over this. Get angry, but don't lose sleep over it. Having said that, I agree, it's now well beyond a joke. We've got to do something.'

'I know, that's why I want to challenge Cuff. He must prove it's not him.'

'Actually, that's the wrong way round. It's you who has to prove it *is* him.'

She should be coming to me by now, but she's still not responding to my messages of love. I must do more to engage her in close conversation, which will slide smoothly into face-to-face contact. I don't think she realises my creation has assumed a mind of his own. Soon I won't be able to control him, and it won't be long before he'll be a far greater danger to her. I must explain the threat he poses in very clear terms and how she can prevent the otherwise inevitable damage.

An intrusion, a clamour demanding her attention. Sleep shattered. 'What the hell?'

Her mobile phone was lit on the far side of the room. Imogen stumbled out of bed and peered at it; that same number again. 'Bloody hell, it's three in the morning. I'm not answering that.' She put the instrument on the bedside table and crawled back between the sheets. Sleep would be impossible now, and, as if to reinforce that, the ping of a voicemail disturbed her. She switched the phone to silent, pulled the blankets over her head and turned away. Half an hour later, just as she was drifting into sleep, her mobile again vibrated on the table. This time she turned the thing off, but it left her furious, grumpy and thoroughly pissed off, in that order, she concluded.

When she switched the phone back on at six thirty there were a string of voicemails to show he'd called every half hour. The only satisfaction was that the bastard had lost more sleep than she had. At seven on the dot there was another call. This time she accepted it but said nothing.

Once again the only sound was faint breathing. To respond to this sinister noise would be an invitation to him. Let Cuff run up his phone bill. She put the instrument next to her Lily doll, then cut a slice of bread and put it in the toaster. She peered at the screen. The call was still connected, but the stalker was silent. As the toaster popped with its distinctive metallic sound, a soft and distorted voice said, 'I'm sorry that happened. I love you so much, I need you so much. I'll protect you from him. Give me time to sort it out. I'm watching over you.'

Imogen shook her head; this was so confusing. *What is driving this clown? Is he dangerous? Is he saying there are actually two men out there?* She switched on the kettle for a second cup of coffee, took the milk out of the fridge and looked at the phone again. The call had been terminated.

Showered, dressed and ready to go, she took a last look at her bloodshot and red-rimmed eyes in the mirror and shrugged. *If anyone thinks I look rough, I couldn't give a damn. And if anyone so much as dares to comment, I'll bite their head off and prove their point.*

At her feet on the top step lay another box of Thornton's chocolates. She picked them up and put them on the hall table, then went out and made sure the front door was locked. Facing the street again, she froze, and gaped. Her bike lay discarded on top of the hedge. The security chain had been chopped through and was lying on the ground. One of the wheels was buckled, and both tyres had been shredded. The saddle was slashed.

Tears of anger and frustration at this stupid destruction threatened to flow. She forced them down. *What is this idiot hoping to achieve by wrecking my things?*

When she heard, Melissa sounded just as angry at the

news. 'I'm moving in with you. Don't even think of arguing about it. This man is proving violent, and two of us together have a much better chance of being safe than you alone.'

'No, I'll be fine, I—'

'I said, don't argue. I'll bring my things round this evening.'

'It's weird, Melissa, I think there might be two men involved.'

'What?'

8

18 July

The twins walked ahead of him. Occasionally they broke into a trot, then skipped like eight-year-olds, then walked again. They chatted in German and giggled and held hands, and would turn back to see how he was doing.

'I'm good,' Cuff called in response. *Sometimes I feel like a paedophile instead of being the sex slave of twenty-five-year-olds.*

He had never been in these woods before and had no idea where the path led. From the car, the track climbed a gentle slope below the trees and continued up towards the top of the ridge. The picnic hamper was a pain to carry, not heavy, but awkward, and it lengthened the journey. He held it out in front of him because the girls had insisted it be kept level. They had an easier time with light daypacks which sagged from something small in them.

'So we are here, Cuff. You like it?'

They emerged from the dimness of the woods into a grey day with darkening clouds. A clear grassy area near the top of the hill gave an unlimited view to the south. Was that the sea in the distance? Coming closer, the rolling countryside spread out before him. Hedge-bound fields, herds and flocks and two old farms a mile apart. A church steeple was the only evidence of a tiny village otherwise hidden amongst trees. Immediately below him was a disused quarry. The top of the far wall was well below him. He went to the edge and looked down the sheer cliff into a dark pool of water.

The twins stood behind him. 'Be careful, Cuff. Maybe the edge is not safe.'

Nervous giggles.

Anna opened her pack and pulled out a red gingham cloth. Cuff sat on the grass beside it, while Hannah open the hamper. The sight of cheese, *wurst*, sauerkraut, tomatoes and cold meats to go with a dark and heavy-looking bread made his mouth water. He settled three goblets into the grass and opened the wine.

'Cheers, girls.'

'*Prost*, Cuff,' they answered in unison.

'This is a great spot for a picnic. How did you find it?'

'We were walking, actually. There is a ruin through there, in the trees. It is interesting. We are not sure what it was. You should go and see while we prepare the feast, and you can tell us some history after.'

'Okay. I could do with a private stroll anyway.'

'I can't find a ruin,' Cuff said when he came back.

'Never mind, we will show you later. First we feed our man, yes?'

'Yes.'

One patted the ground beside her. 'Sit here, Cuff, between us. We go home tomorrow and we want to make the most of you.'

'Maybe we never meet again,' the other said.

'We must not be sad, this is not the time. Eat up, then we have more wine and make great sex out here in the open to celebrate and to remember.'

'We can't do that here. Someone might see us. This is a public place. You're going, but I have to live here.'

The girls giggled. 'Cuff, if someone comes and sees, they will run away. They will be shocked, and we can carry on. Maybe a man will see and think he can make it equal numbers. We will take care of him. It is not necessary to worry about this. You must relax and enjoy what we have cooked up for you – something very different.'

'Relax? I feel very relaxed; sleepy, in fact.' His torso swayed. To his left. Anna, if it was her, was blurred. Hannah, on his right, was also fuzzy. He blinked, trying to clear his head. Smiles on either side. Smiles of friendship, or …?

'Are you okay, Cuff? You look a little white, actually. Lie down.'

He let his body fall back to the grass and closed his eyes. His hands were brought together in front of him. Something coarse went around his wrists – and was tightened.

'Hey, what are you doing?' His fear of restraint rushed up and gave him some clarity. He sat upright again, tugged and twisted. Thick, old-style hemp rope was wound around his wrists and over itself, tightening the loops. Hannah held the end.

'A little game only. We are cuffing Cuff.' They both laughed, but it didn't sound humorous.

'One more thing, Cuff.'

The view, the sun, the fresh air; suddenly it was all gone. A bag was rammed over his head.

Panic. *What's going on? What are they doing? Why? I can't breath! Rubbish, I can. Control. I must control myself. I must stay calm. Not so easy, when I can't stop panting and my heart is breaking out of my chest.* His greatest fear – and he had told them what it was.

Humourless tittering.

Sleep was trying to drag him to another place. He struggled to fight the drug's effect. Something was very wrong. There was more to fear in this than a mere bag.

'It's not funny. Take this off. *Take it off now.*' His voice was high-pitched, squeaky, the threat in it ineffective.

'Wait.'

Was the drug wearing off already? His senses were slowly coming back to him. A hand on his shoulder held him down. The other twin moved away. A long pause. His mind raced, but found no solution. She came back. Hands were under his elbows, lifting him. They propelled him forward.

Where?

He had been sitting facing the quarry.

'What are you doing?'

They pushed.

He dropped. A violent wrench to his arms. His weight nearly tore them from their sockets. His bagged head smacked back against the rock face. It hurt, which didn't matter. But his feet were dangling freely in space. He was in trouble – big trouble.

The bag was whipped off. Facing outward, his view returned: the distant sea, fields, animals, the village and its church steeple. He couldn't turn away from it. And below his feet – a clear drop.

'What's going on? What are you doing? Pull me up.'

'No, Cuff. You are tied to a tree. Very soon we are going to cut the rope around your wrists and you are going to fall into the water. Maybe you hit some rocks on the way down. It's a long way, maybe thirty metres. About the same as for Rolfy.'

'Who the fuck's Rolfy?'

'Barry Rolf Castle was our cousin. He would do anything for us; he loved us. Our Auntie Eva loved him. You killed him.'

'Barry Castle? For God's sake. That was an accident. They said so at the inquest. I did not kill him, I tried to save him, even after he tried to kill me.'

'That is too bad, Cuff. It is your bad luck we are against you, because even if we believed you did not kill him, we like very much to have great sex then kill our mates – true Black Widows, actually.'

'You are number three. We are keeping a score. We cut a little mark in our bedheads at home every time.'

Once again they giggled. This time it was genuine: a weird, dark humour.

A dog barked. Another yapped excitedly. A whistle pierced the air.

Cuff screamed, '*Help.*'

'It's too late, Cuff.' The voice was almost a whisper, inches above his head.

The dogs were closer, a constant yapping and deeper barking.

Four blue eyes, void of any emotion, gazed down at his upturned face. 'It was great sex. A pity, it has to end like this, but you did kill Rolf.'

'*Help.*'

'Quickly, Anna, cut the rope. We must go. No, wait. I want to look into his eyes as he goes, to watch the life go out of him, like we always do.'

'*Help.*'

The dogs were there, scuffling and sniffing.

Hannah snapped at them in German. The bigger dog growled, the little one yapped louder, then squealed in pain.

'Hey! That's my dog, you bloody bitch.' A deep voice.

Something was scratching the bonds at his wrists. He

stretched his head back to see. The knife was at the rope, and a few strands were free. Two heads he'd thought were pretty were hideous now.

'Hey!' The same deep voice, closer now.

Suddenly the heads were gone. Sounds of scurrying and running.

'Aargh! You fucking bitch.'

Cuff looked up. The cut in the rope was between his wrists, neat and clean, but it was only halfway through. *Will it hold? Where's that man? Has he been stabbed?*

'Help.'

A dog whimpered; someone groaned. No one appeared above him.

The grogginess stayed with him. *It's weaker than it was, but I can't shake it off entirely. I must think clearly, there's no hope in irrational thought.*

The slightest jerk, the smallest tug might be enough to part the rope. As carefully as he could, Cuff used his legs to turn so he faced the cliff. This was not a time for weakness. He tried to grip the rope in case it failed, but his hands were in the wrong position and had no strength.

He put his feet to the rock and, leaning back on the rope, walked his way up the face. That was easy. He still had to pull his upper body in to the cliff top. His arms had been stretched out, they were short of blood and weak. Without being able to use his hands further along the rope, he would only be able to pull himself in by the length of his upper arms. He walked his feet higher until they were firmly planted on safe ground and he was almost horizontal in space. He had to summon the strength. It had to be done quickly to get enough momentum to carry him onto the grass. If only he could grip the rope.

This was not going to work. It was mechanically

impossible. Instead, his feet had to find a firm grip lower down the face. The longer he took, the weaker he would get. One foot found a secure hold. He delved around with the other. A piece of rock came away. It caused a jerk. The cut in the rope looked no worse. He tried again; tested both feet. They felt firm – they had to be firm.

He carefully pulled himself in to the rock. His weight came onto his feet. The strain on his shoulders eased a little. He was still hanging backwards, but a lot closer to the cliff. Somehow he had to get hold of the rope ahead of him to make any further progress. He might be able to pull a little further so he could grip the rope with his teeth. Would he be able to hold his body weight using his teeth?

'*Bloody hell*. Hang on, mate. Hang on, I'll pull you in. Aagh!'

9

21–25 July

Cuff was pressing his uniform for the next day, having made a tentative attempt to clean the flat while listening to Pink Floyd. The music was background, flowing over him, immersing him. He would be history now if luck hadn't struck with the arrival of a man and his dogs. His rescuer had been wounded and his little terrier bloodied – neither seriously. They had walked with difficulty down to meet the rescue services, Cuff carrying the dog, the man holding his side, and the larger Labrador staying protectively close.

What had happened to the twins? They were a determined pair, they were single minded about killing him to avenge Barry Castle – or Rolf, as they called him. Would they return, or had they left the country? Cuff had reported the incident and the dog walker had supported him, so the police would be looking for them and would have alerted the German police or Europol, so H-Anna would be on the run. But Cuff knew he would have to be vigilant while they were still at large.

Ginny had said he should follow his natural instincts and act as his alter ego, 'Jonathan', would. He'd agreed and was doing that, but discovered he didn't have to actively look for stimulation – it found him.

Housework was boring. What with the ironing, and his flat being on the top floor, it was hot with the sun beating down on the roof. He had the window open, but the air was still and stifling. It would be much more enjoyable to go over to Casewell for some aerobatics, especially if Sonia was free to join him.

The rap on the door was angry and determined. It was not the hesitant knock of a caller who was worried about disturbing the occupant. *Hell, is it H-Anna?*

He peered through the spy hole and relaxed.

'Hello, ladies,' Cuff said. 'This is unexpected. Come in. Sorry about the books all over the place, I'm in lecture preparation mode.'

'Cuff,' both girls said curtly.

What on earth are they doing here? And they look seriously pissed off. He closed the door behind them. The track switched from 'Is There Anybody Out There?' to 'One Of My Turns'. He turned the volume down.

'Cuff, are you stalking me?'

His eyes widened. 'What?' His mouth stayed open.

'Are you stalking me? It's a simple question.'

'Good grief – no. What on earth makes you think that?' *Where the hell did this come from?*

'I've been getting suggestive texts immediately after you've sent one – I've seen you.'

'That must be pure coincidence. It doesn't mean I'm

stalking you, for heaven's sake.'

'Which is my flat?' Imogen stabbed a finger through the open window at the house across the road.

'I haven't a clue. I know you live there, but which flat …? You're being incredibly aggressive, Imogen. Why don't you relax a little and have a coffee?'

'No.' She was leaning towards him, glaring, with her clenched fists planted firmly on her hips.

'Yes please,' said Melissa. She put a hand on Imogen's arm. 'Put your hackles down, Imo. Sit and take the coffee. We need to discuss this rationally.'

Cuff stood looking at the pair for a moment and waiting for Imogen to say yea or nay to his offer. He shrugged, left them to it and switched on the kettle.

'Have you got a camera?' Imogen was still standing with her back to the couch. Melissa had found a chair.

'Yes.' He took his old Leica out of a cupboard and handed it to her. The kettle gave its irritating beep. 'Change your mind about the coffee?'

'Oh, all right. Yes.' Imogen sat at last, and with the action, relaxed a little. She stared at the small but heavy camera with interest. 'Do you have a bigger one, or a long lens for this?'

'No, on both counts. That's a rangefinder camera. I think the longest lens for it is 135mm, but I don't have one. Why?'

'How do I look at the pictures on this thing?'

'You can't. It's a film camera. I like film, especially black-and-white. Why?'

'Because photos of me in my flat, directly opposite this one, have been pushed through my letterbox. The photos were taken from here, on this level. They're very high quality and high magnification.'

Cuff handed the girls their coffees. The faint odour of Imogen's scent hung over her. Alluring, it was the same one she always wore. Siren-like, it tried to entice him closer. He stood back, away from its influence. 'Imogen, I don't know what to say, other than it wasn't me. Are you sure they were taken from this flat? Not next door?'

'They're from a position that's directly opposite, as I said.'

'Not the roof? It's just there.' He pointed up to the ceiling.

'The roof? Nobody's going to sit on a sloping roof and take pictures.'

'Why not? This is a Georgian building. The roof is not visible from the street, it's low and set back behind a parapet. Once you're up there, you can walk around the pitched roof itself immediately behind the parapet wall.' Again his hand traced a pathway along the outside edge of the ceiling.

'Oh – I suppose that's possible. But you're not the person you want people to believe you are.'

Cuff's eyes narrowed and his voice was sharp. 'I'm not sure I like your approach. You'd better explain that.'

'I Googled you.'

'Ah. You've discovered my despicable past, have you? Not that it's any of your business, Imogen.'

'Of course it's my business. I put my trust in you, I put my life in your hands. I discover you're stalking me, and then find out what sort of man you really are – not very nice: violent, unfaithful, a womaniser and possibly a murderer. That makes it my business – definitely.'

Cuff returned her angry stare with his own. 'It is none of your business, but, to put your mind at ease and enable you to continue flying with me, I'll tell you what really happened.'

'I'm never flying with you again. I'll join another school, and I'm going to the police about you.'

Melissa put her arm round Imogen's shoulders and pulled her close. 'Imo, you must calm yourself. There are two sides to every story, and you have to hear Cuff's.'

Imogen said nothing, but put her head down. When she

raised it again, she wiped an angry tear away. 'Go on, then.'

'Would you like something stronger? This is a long story.'

'Yes please,' Melissa said eagerly. She stood, followed him to the fridge and spoke softly. 'Cuff, Imo's pretty shaken by this stalking thing, and she's reacting badly. Have some patience, please.'

He told them almost everything, fielding questions as he went. He didn't get as far as Friday's brush with death.

'You got divorced because of your affair with a woman in accounts.'

'Not true. Lisa wanted to believe it to give herself an excuse for her own infidelity. Why did you call me a womaniser, anyway?'

'Well, there was your affair, you've shown an interest in me which led to you stalking me, you found those blonde sisters, and you still showed an interest in me while going with them. That's womanising.'

'Twins, actually, and they found me. And what right do you have to call me a womaniser for having a fling with some girls when I'm single? After all, you're having a relationship with Mike Penny, which is something I have difficulty understanding.'

'Touché,' said Melissa. She had a naughty expression on her face, as if she found the spat between the other two entertaining.

Cuff pulled his sleeves up enough to show them the rope burns on his wrists. 'The twins episode did not end well.'

'What are those marks? No, don't tell me, I don't want to know about your weird tastes. You've a sick mind. And it's another sign pointing to you as the stalker.'

'Okay, now I'm losing my patience with you. You come marching in here accusing me of something without any reasonable proof. You've dug into my past and found the worst things to believe. You will not listen to my explanations. You're determined I'm guilty, and now you're insinuating I'm perverted. I'm not, but even if I were, it's none of your damned business!'

Melissa stood, turned and faced her friend. 'Imo, he's right. That was out of line, and you're being completely unreasonable.'

Imogen sat staring vacantly at the floor. Her jaw muscles were working as if she was debating on issuing an apology. Melissa tugged at her arm. 'Come on, we should go. Sorry, Cuff.'

He opened the front door for them. 'Will you go to the police?'

Imogen did not raise her head. She seemed incapable of answering. Melissa took over. 'No, she wants to catch him herself. She doesn't think the police will take her seriously.'

'If you take them your phone with the texts, and you show them the photos, and if I come with you and hand over my phone for them to analyse, I'm sure they'll take you seriously, and you'll see it wasn't me who sent your messages.'

Imogen lifted her head and gave him a defiant glare. 'You could have used another phone.'

'I'm not sure what I've done to deserve this, but you're determined to pin this on me, aren't you?'

My photos of her naked beauty started the rot. They have ruined her self-confidence.

She saw him from her window as he waited for her in the street, watching for a sign – did she sleep after that? He destroyed her bike and ripped her tyres, taking this to a different and nerve-wracking level. He's becoming more and more sinister, and he'll wear her down eventually.

He will have her truly frightened, running, looking behind her at every corner, scanning the street before she ventures out – who is following her? He wants her to feel naked and unprotected in a wild and dangerous world before he strikes. She's not quite ready yet to beg for help. When she does, and she will, that will be the time to present myself as her saviour and bring her under my protection.

Already she's looking around everywhere as if she's scared, and I can't blame her. Her friend has moved in. Is that because she's nervous or because she likes girls? With that other woman in her flat, he's likely to be so despicable as to tell the world she's a lesbian. All she has to do to avoid that scandal is succumb to my will, that's all.

Imogen led the way back into her flat. She went directly to the window and pulled the curtains closed even though it was still mid-afternoon.

'Why?'

'Because he can see in, and because I feel like hiding from the world.'

'You're letting this get to you. We need to bring it to a head and stop it. You have got to go to the police, Imo. Let them handle it. They'll interview Cuff and tell you whether he's a threat or not.'

'The police don't want to believe women. Look it up – I have. There's child grooming cases going on from 2005 at least, with the police simply not believing the girls. Why should they believe me, a grown woman who's so far unhurt? No, I want to catch this bastard myself, and it's a lot easier now I know who he is.'

'Imo, humour me. It's going to do no harm to report the stalking and tell the police you suspect him. What are you going to do about your flying?'

'I can't fly with him any more, not after what I said today, can I? There's no way I can have another instructor at Fernbury. Mike is an absolute no-no, and besides, he can't fly at the moment. There's only one thing to do and that's to find another school. Connor said Casewell is at capacity, but I'll check anyway. If I can't get in there I'll have to move further away. Maybe I should do that anyway – get out of this clown's sight and reach.'

'I don't want you to move away. I need you, Imo.'

'Oh, Melissa. You're so bloody sensible; and I need you too – desperately. Come here, I need a shoulder to cry on.'

Imogen broke the hug, but held her friend at arm's length. 'I've got time to think. As it happens, Old Ma Mavis wants me back again for a week. She says she's got piles of dictation for me, so I won't be able to fly anyway.'

'Is she someone you can lean on?'

'I think so. She's a wise old owl and has quite a history as a war correspondent. Underneath her fragile exterior, she's a toughie. I might try. I tell you what, if she also tells me to go to the police, I will.'

Detective Inspector Williams listened carefully to Imogen's complaint and to Melissa's occasional input. There was no messing about, no suave detectives chatting up pretty constables or groups of men clustered round a computer screen avidly watching something they shouldn't. Every single person was busy, and some were even flustered.

'You should have come to me a good bit earlier,' the DI said.

'I didn't want to, because I thought you wouldn't take me seriously.'

Williams sighed. 'Unfortunately, some of my colleagues still do not see the gravity of these complaints. However, you're in luck in that my niece was stalked, and I saw it was serious. The poor girl was terrified. Mind you, the texts and acts were a lot worse than you've been exposed to.' He looked pointedly at Imogen. 'Suffice to say, I got the, er … perpetrator. So I do believe you, and we'll find this man, or woman. If you let me have your phone for a moment, I'll get the number the texts were sent from and we'll see if we can trace it. Usually, though, stalkers use pay-as-you-go SIM cards and we can't identify the owner from them. But what they don't realise is, with every call the IMEI number is sent as well. That's a unique number allocated to a particular phone, so we can trace its origin and often find the culprit from there.'

Imogen passed her phone across the desk.

'Thank you. I'll interview Mr Scott and we'll see where it takes us. This has to be handled carefully, because if he hasn't been doing these things, you could wreck his reputation and damage his future. So before I arrest anyone I'm going to have to be very sure of my ground. And I warn you, it's not easy to prove this kind of thing. I'll keep you advised of progress. Don't be shy to notify me immediately if you think you face an imminent threat.'

DI Williams was apologetic. As he had predicted, the SIM card was a pay-as-you-go type and not traceable to anyone, but the IMEI number revealed that the phone had been bought by a Pakistani man in Leeds five years ago. The man had died a year later, and the phone had been sold to an unknown person through a small-time dealer. The detective asked Imogen to let him know as soon as the stalker made his next move.

Imogen joined Melissa in the park after hearing from Williams. They had talked about little other than the stalking ever since it began. It was controlling her life; sad, but it was what it was: important.

'Williams has interviewed Cuff. Having analysed his phone and the telephone company records, he said he has no evidence that Cuff is the stalker, but he's got no evidence to point a finger at anyone else either. Cuff is still the biggest red spot on my radar, though. It could be one of the students, but how would he know my phone number and where I live? He would have to go through the staff files to find that out. The only other likely person is Mike. He was always trying to control me, always manipulating me, and maybe now he's so annoyed I've dumped him, he's increasing the pressure. That would explain his attitude that I belong to him. It fits – but so much of this is not his style. And we mustn't forget there might be two of them.'

Melissa's reply was stalled by Imogen's phone pinging a message. She pulled it from her hip pocket and read the words. Her mouth narrowed into a tiny oval shape.

'She's in our way and must go. My lips kiss the creamy skin of your thigh, moving gently upwards, tantalising. Even now your breathing shortens in anticipation.'

'Disgusting bastard.'

'Remember Imo, this stalking started before you dumped Mike. Don't be so hasty in blaming him.'

Imogen glanced at her. 'He lives in the same building as Cuff. He can see my window. The photos weren't taken from his flat, but he would have known when to take them. He's in a firm second place.'

Imogen sorted her mail after returning from typing Old Ma Mavis's manuscript all afternoon. Five junk items: she didn't reckon she was ready for a retirement home just yet; the pizzas that crowd sent were terrible last time she tried them; Oxfam; a cruise to the Caribbean – no thanks, too inactive; and a local chimney sweep when she didn't have a chimney. Finally, a letter addressed to her, but not Miss or Ms or even her surname, only IMOGEN and the address. *Odd, it must be from someone who knows me, but none of my friends writes a letter these days.*

She turfed the junk into the recycling and took the letter to the table. Her hand went up to cover her mouth. *This can't be happening to me.* Sitting back she pushed the page away. A brief wave of nausea hit her. The muscles in her neck were tense and painful.

As soon as Melissa walked in the door, Imogen handed her the letter without commenting. Melissa read aloud, and without the joking she so often employed.

'This was done on an old typewriter with a rather tired ribbon. Courier font. Who has one of those these days?

'My Darling Imo,

Texts are simply not adequate to express what I have to say to you. This letter provides an in-depth background to what I feel and what we can do about our future in ways which cannot possibly be done in 160 characters of text. I will still text you to keep you up to date, but use this letter as the source of information you can refer to if in doubt (although there should never be doubt in your mind).

I can call you Imo, can't I? Your best friends call you that, not Imogen, which is too long. Imo is more familiar, too, and the point where our familiarity reached the intimate is long passed. I know I can call you Imo, because I am so much more than your best friend; I am your lover. Not a lover in the common sense of the word as it refers to a sleeping partner, but a person who loves you unconditionally and unequivocally.

Believe it.

I feel God has brought you to me, presented you to me in all your beauty. I use the word 'beauty' in a way that encompasses all its aesthetic references: your form, your features, your intellect, your physical appearance, your glistening thick hair fashioned in such a carefree manner so as to express your wild and unrestrained nature — so sensual. That mole on your inner thigh; I have a similar one and long to caress yours. See, we are destined to be joined. I worship you as a child of God, as a young woman of intelligence and determination and skill.

Skill, you ask? Yes, I hear you're learning to fly, and very well. How brave and independent for a woman. One day you will be flying me to New York as I recline behind you and sip champagne, confident in the knowledge that the very best pair of hands and the very best brain has control over my life for a few hours.

I worship and admire you. You rise above all other women, and many men, with your attributes. I do not like feminism, but I do want to see the underdogs of this sorry world break free from the chains which hold back talent. You are a leader, a torchbearer for such people. You are an example to all, including those who are already successful. In fact, those who have been rewarded with an easy path to their goal in life should look up to you.

You should be in no doubt as to my love for you. I yearn for the day when we can be together and we will lie together. I will take you in my arms and make love to you until we are sated. We will explore our bodies and our sex every which way, in every possible locale and at all times of the day and night. You will love me and find you will not be able to do without me. As your working day passes, you will be unable to concentrate for your desire and actual need to be with me, to be beneath me, to satisfy me and to serve me.

Our life will be idyllic, but there is a journey to take before we get there, Imo my love. You have to come to me. I have already made my commitment to you, now it is your turn to give yourself unconditionally to me.

Otherwise.

`There is another man.'`

She read the rest of the page in silence. 'Blah-di-blah. This second half is a bit scary, but it does remind us to be ultra-careful. Mike didn't write this, you know.'

'I agree, but why do you say that?'

'Mike doesn't talk like this. This is someone who has a better command of English than he does.'

'Cuff. It always comes back to Cuff.'

'Not necessarily. Whoever it is has created another person to enforce his will over you. There's a physical presence which is threatening, and a loving one who calls and texts you. The question might be whether he knows what he's created or whether he believes there is another.'

'So he's either delusional or evil?'

'Or both. One thing's for sure, you've got to take this threat of physical harm seriously. We're going to—'

'Of course I'm taking it seriously. Why the hell do you think I'm sitting here with a face like thunder?'

'Calm down, Imo, please. I was going to say, we must have a solid plan, and the first thing is to ensure you stay safe.'

'Sorry, I'm a bit wound up.'

Melissa stood behind her friend and massaged her neck. 'You must not go out alone. I'm going to be with you outside this flat whenever possible, and we must take that letter to Inspector Williams straightaway. You can't hide in constant fear of an acid attack or something, but you have to stay vigilant of the people around you. I'll be with you until this bastard is caught.'

10

01–10 August

Imogen was gazing absently out of her window at the road below. The sun had set, and the moon was new and could not be seen. The orange light of dusk was fading into the blackness of night. She closed the curtains.

'Today's the first of August. I went to the police on the twenty-second. Before then, there were messages about every two or three days, but since reporting it I've had a barrage of texts from this creep. There's been one every day; some days there have even been two. They are getting more and more disgusting and bordering on obscene. It's all suggestive stuff, a bunch of soft words which translate crudely into "I'm going to fuck you". He's even hinting at positions. I thought I would become immune to them, but he's chipping away at me, trying to get me to submit to his will through a mixture of adoration and sexual innuendo. He's failing, because although I am tiring of it all, I'm not getting weaker, I'm getting more and more pissed off. If I ever get to meet him, he'll know just how pissed off I am.'

Melissa was once again hogging the whole of Imogen's little couch, with her feet up on one of the arms, her back against the other and a glass of wine in her hand. 'You've already met him, you just don't know who he is.'

Imogen turned back to face her friend and shrugged. 'True. It's got to be Cuff. But how do I prove it?'

'Whoever it is, and I'm betting you it's not Cuff, he'll slip up somehow. You'll have to keep a stiff upper lip until the opportunity arises to nail him.'

Imogen paced up and down the cramped room with short, urgent steps. 'And I'm going to be the one who does that.'

'Settle down, girl,' Melissa urged. 'You'll give yourself a stress fracture of the heart or brain or something, and I'm only allowed to nurse animals, not humans. You must learn to accept this tripe. It's a bit of turbulence in your life. Ride it out. Don't let it worry you so much. It will die out, or he'll eventually be caught.'

Imogen was at the window again. She drew the curtain back a little. 'He's there again! Under the lamp post. Put your shoes on, we're going to get the bastard.'

'You stay there so he can see you, and I'll go out and get behind him. As soon as you see me, come and join me.'

'You'll be on your own too long. No.'

Melissa pulled a long carver out of the kitchen drawer. 'I'm taking one of your knives.'

'No, no knife. That's stupid, it's too dangerous.'

'It's only to threaten him, to keep him at bay. See you down there.'

Imogen's heart pounded; this situation could turn nasty, because Melissa was fearless.

The man was wearing his hat and looking up from beneath the street light, his face in shadow, his unseen eyes locked on hers as before. Imogen held the curtain back so he could see her face, hoping his attention would be held while Melissa came up behind him. *What is she going to do? How is she going to tackle this man? What if he overpowers her and turns the knife on her instead?*

Melissa had gone out of the back door and through the garden. Her friend appeared some thirty yards behind the stalker. Imogen's nails dug into her palms. Dropping the curtain, she sprinted for the stairs, running a hand down the banister, nearly falling once. With the front door cracked open, she peered out. Melissa was getting close. There was no time for delay.

Imogen stepped outside. He saw her and turned his body away, but still he watched her. Melissa had ten yards to go. She was holding the knife out ahead, pointing it at him, her steps cat-like and soft.

Cuff glanced across the street. Imogen's curtains were closed but the light was on. He had not seen her at the school since she had accused him over a week ago. Surely she had not given up on flying? Probably looking for another school – that was a shame, and so unnecessary.

Odd – down on the road a man was standing under one of the street lamps. Why, on a warm night in August, would you wear a long coat and a hat? He was apparently staring up at Imogen's flat, or maybe the other one on the first floor.

Was this Imogen's stalker? If he was, he wasn't doing anything, merely standing there.

Cuff's eye was caught by a movement from the back of Imogen's house. Long, bouncy fair hair – Melissa. She was creeping low along the hedge to get to the road. A glint of something in her hand. A memory of a big man with a long knife spurred him into action.

No! No, Melissa. That's not the way.

Imogen was coming out of the front door. *You stupid women. Someone's going to get hurt.*

Cuff rammed his feet into his shoes. Grabbed his keys, shot out of the door, took the stairs two at a time. Opened the front door quietly, crept down the path. The man's back was to him.

Melissa was ten yards up the road to his right, the knife out in front of her.

Imogen was about to cross the road.

The man was turning away, preparing to run, but keeping a watch on her.

Melissa scuffed a foot. He heard it, snapped his head round, saw the knife and bolted.

Cuff leapt the knee-high garden wall.

Imogen tried to cut off the man's retreat, her arms out wide. A sidestep as neat as a rugby centre, and he dodged her.

Cuff sprinted past her. A diving tackle. His arms clamped the lower legs. The man was down, fighting. Cuff lost his grip, but caught the coat in one hand. The man was on his feet again. He kicked out. Connected. Ripped his coat free.

He was gone.

Cuff, on his hands and knees, spat blood onto the pavement. Melissa held out her hand, but he clambered to his feet without help.

'Thanks, Cuff. Are you okay?'

'Fine, Melissa. Are you two all right?'

Imogen was looking at him, studying him. She was in silhouette with the street lamp behind her, but she was being no more friendly than before. 'Thank you, Cuff,' she murmured.

'Well, that lays your suspicions to rest, doesn't it, Imo? It wasn't Cuff who was watching you.'

'I told you, I think there's two of them. One playing nice, and that was the nasty one.'

Cuff sucked on the blood in his mouth. One tooth was loose. 'What are you talking about – two of them?'

Imogen said nothing. Melissa explained.

Cuff said, 'It's not likely to be two people – that's a long shot. It's more likely one man creating a situation where the nice one rescues you from the nasty one.'

'Any ideas who?'

'He looked tall in the coat and hat, but he was short really. He moved quickly. If Mike hadn't hurt his ankle, I would've said it was him.'

Sonia woke to the happy twittering of birds outside the window. She raised her head and, for a while, watched a robin on the sill. It flew away, she couldn't. *How lucky that bird is to be free from all the constraints of being a human: having dependents, emotional ties, financial restrictions.* Oh, how she needed to follow it!

She eased out of bed, taking care not to disturb the sleeping body beside her, slipped on a gown and went to the bathroom. Opening the robe in front of the mirror, she ran her hands over her body, stroking the flatness of her stomach; the tautness of her skin, devoid of any trace of fat, which failed to soften the outline of her hip bones and ribs; and her small breasts which had never known a child. She lifted a leg. The muscles in her thigh reacted like tensioned straps beneath the sparse flesh. It wasn't the first time she had asked herself if the sight was ugly or something to be proud of – this product of being a long-distance runner.

With the coffee machine filled with water, and milk in the frother, she looked around what used to be the kitchen she shared with him. What would life be like now if she and

Connor had stayed together? There had been several reasons leading them to realise it was the best thing for both of them to separate. Even so, she resented the way he had treated her, discarding her without displaying any emotion whatsoever. Brushing her off as if picking a speck of fluff from his jacket. It could have been much more amicable. If it had, she would come to him now with kindness and affection and leave fulfilled, both emotionally and physically. But now, with the lack of sentiment in their relationship, her departure was accompanied only by guilt, as if she had hired a gigolo to bring her satisfaction in the only way open to her.

How did Connor view these irregular sessions? Were they purely an avenue for release, as if he was visiting a prostitute? Maybe he did that, too? Did he also regret she was not with him every night so love could be made whenever the desire took them, instead of making elaborate arrangements to stay or go to the hotel on special occasions?

These same thoughts went through her mind every time she came here. And each time she ended up feeling used, like a whore to be discarded in the morning. She would never forgive him for treating her this way, but her physical need built up over a couple of weeks to overcome her sensitivities.

The kettle boiled and Sonia dashed some water into the mugs to preheat them. While she waited she glanced along the counter at Connor's neat arrangement. His iPad, phone, camera, wallet and keys were stacked in line against the side of the fridge, a one-inch gap separating each item. So typical of him – hers were all over the place. Half the time she could not find whatever it was she needed, whereas he knew exactly where he'd put everything.

She put a spoon of sugar in Connor's mug, nothing in hers, then put a capsule into the machine. With the second mug ready, she only had to wait for the frother to finish.

What was Connor doing with himself in his personal time

since she left? She took the two steps necessary to reach the end of the counter.

There had been no text messages, no man watching Imogen from the street, no one following in her footsteps and no phone calls made since they had tried to catch the stalker. There hadn't been a squeak out of him for over a week, and Imogen was beginning to think they had frightened him off. But at three o'clock in the morning of Saturday the ninth, her phone gave its distinctive message tone.

'Why did your friend try to kill him? He is angry about that. I know you came out to protect him. You opened your arms to him, but he had to flee that knife.' And then a second text: *'I saw it all, I'm watching over you. I'm sorry you were frightened my lovely girl.'*

'Oh no, it's starting again. God, I'm tired of this man. We've got to find him very bloody quickly.'

The third text had her shaking her head. *'Soon there will be another time for us, my lovely. We will make love from dusk 'til dawn. I am tireless, I feel your body arching under me, even now.'*

Ten miles into her training, Sonia was breathing easily even though her vest was soaked with sweat. She had not yet covered half the length of a marathon and her plan for the day was for twenty-five miles, which would take some three hours and fifty minutes. The rhythm of running, and the satisfaction of being able to cover so much distance in a respectable time, always soothed her troubles and occasionally enabled her to find solutions to some.

Her mother was one, now in need of full-time care, and being moved into a different home. After buying her own food, all of Sonia's pitiful income went into paying for the care, and the new home was going to be an even greater drain. Time and again, as her feet pounded out their rhythm on the road, ways to increase her earnings surfaced, but had dived back into the depths of impracticality by the end of her run.

Her thoughts turned to Connor – specifically their relationship and break-up. A long time ago when they were a couple, there had been no mention of marriage, but to her there was an unspoken agreement that they would always be together. That was until he erupted one day, out of the blue, moaning about her lack of organisation, her untidiness, her general sloppiness. But that's what she was, a naturally scruffy person who directed all her energies and her limited talent for precision into her flying and everything connected with aviation. There was nothing left to grant to other activities. He had accepted that from the word go – why rebel against her traits after two years?

They had gone their own ways for a while, she smarting from his rejection and he relieved of the burden of having her cluttering his life. After a few weeks he had invited her to dinner in what she thought – hoped – was an attempt to make up. But it wasn't. They drank too much, and her reluctance to forgive his callous treatment of her fell away. They ended up back in bed, an aspect which had always been good. Since then, they had met whenever their abstinence wore out. It was an emotionless congress which did nothing for them other than release their frustrations, as her feet reminded her now, landing one in front of the other, over and over and over again in an endless beat. Neither of them had anyone else; this old rekindled partnership served purely to keep loneliness at bay for a few hours.

Since the first cup of coffee last Sunday morning, though, everything had changed and her life had taken a significant turn for the better. She had carried her discovery upstairs with his steaming mug.

'What do you think you're doing?' she had asked.

Connor's reply was sleepy. 'Huh? What?'

Sonia put his mug on the side table and stood over him. 'This! I'm going to tell the police what you're doing. It's illegal.'

He sat up, his face puffy from sleep. His eyes widened as he saw what she was showing him. His words came rapidly, piling on top of each other. 'No, that's not what you think it is. I can explain. Why would you want to haul me before the police? Didn't you enjoy last night? Our other nights?'

'Connor. You treat me like an escort. You used me in the past, and you use me now. You pay me a pittance on which I battle to survive. I'm an experienced instructor, a true asset to the school, and I'm paid little more than the new boy. A school to which, I might add, I have contributed just as much as you have. You could not have made such a success of it without me.'

His reactions were predictable. He leaned forward off the pillow, the initial alarm in his face replaced by a calculating look.

'Sonia, you're right. I'm sorry, I don't pay you enough, and I'm already in the process of rectifying that. There's no need to bother the police with that stuff, because there's a perfectly valid explanation.'

She smiled without humour. 'Rubbish. For once I hold the whip hand, and I'm going to use it. Think on this: I want a fifty per cent partnership in the school and an income equal to yours. If it means you take a drop in salary to keep the school going, too bad. It's either that, or I'll have you arrested.'

'That's blackmail! You can't do that, you don't deserve a partnership!'

'That's a matter for debate. You had better think what you've been doing and think very carefully about telling me I don't deserve it. This proposal of mine works for both of us.

You stay free, therefore the school doesn't suffer, and I have the same job, but with more responsibility and a better income. If you go to jail, I could still run the school and keep it going until you're released. But when you come out it will be with a reputation, and that won't do the school any good at all. Only I can keep the company running, so a partnership works for both of us. I'll be back in four hours, so you've plenty of time to think.'

What she had not admitted to Connor were her weak points. It would be difficult for her to find another job with so many positive aspects to it. She was deeply attached to the school, having been there since its inception, and did not want to leave. She also did not want Connor to be identified, as he was her only relief from the frustration of being single. And if this arrangement worked out, she would have the upper hand in their relationship. *She* would dictate when and where they met, not him. She would pay the hotel bill every now and again, just to assert her position.

After all, the prospect of another man entering her life had become a fantasy, and she knew accepting the status quo was her best option.

11

13 August

When Cuff had been out to the airfield four weeks ago to try to see what was going on with the night flights, it had been just after midnight on a Wednesday morning. Later that day he had co-opted Martin's help, and for a few days afterwards he had checked the aircraft parking area at around the same time to see if any of the machines were missing. They weren't, which wasn't surprising because it had been cloudy with little light for the landings.

After that, Cuff had often woken late at night and listened, but heard nothing.

On the thirteenth, he joined Ginny and Martin for a pub meal. Returning home at around eleven, he passed the airfield and had a brief look at the parking area.

He phoned Martin. 'The Cessna is missing. I sense

something is about to happen.'

Martin laughed at him. 'Is that you, "Jonathan"? Sorry, I didn't recognise your voice.'

They met in good time to get in position before the little aeroplane returned. Cuff didn't want to take any chances, so both of them wore dark clothing. The night had been clear to start with, but by twelve o'clock a thin cloud layer heralding a warm front from the west crept across the sky. It would soon smother the moon before it set at around one thirty. The silvery light would be banished, not only for the night, but also for the days it would take for the weather to move through.

'I know what he's doing, he's only flying a few days either side of the full moon so he can see the airfield and the approach before he puts his landing lights on. That's why we haven't seen him for a month,' Cuff remarked, before leaving Martin at his chosen position where he could see the runway and the place where the Cessna stopped to unload whatever it was carrying.

'You must keep your distance, Martin, and only use the phone if you're sure you won't be heard. I'll call you as he lands. Then we'll keep the line open until he taxis over to park. I'll switch my ringer off, but probably won't answer if you call, as he's bound to hear me. I'll only be a few yards from him.'

Martin's voice betrayed his excitement. 'Okay, no problem,' he said with a sniff. 'I hope you get to see him.'

Cuff left his friend and once again parked his car at the field gate. He walked briskly past the buildings of the flying school, which looked even darker than they had previously. Connor's car was not there.

He found a position by the hangar which was closer to the Cessna's parking spot than the previous occasion. It would give him a greater chance of seeing the man's face. The spot was vacant, and there were three jerry cans standing against the hangar wall near the corner. The place was set for the pilot to return.

A little after twelve thirty, Cuff rang Martin. 'He's just passed overhead. I can't see him, but he'll turn finals in about a minute.'

Martin replied in a whisper. 'Okay, I'll keep the line open now. Interesting – a van passed here a moment ago, tootling down the road quite slowly. I saw brake lights for a second or two, nothing after that. I think he's gone.'

'Here he comes. Can you hear him?'

'Yeah. I can hear the air as much as the engine. Christ! He leaves it late for the landing light, doesn't he? … He's down … stopping.'

Silence.

'Martin, you there? What's happening? I can't see so well from here.'

'Three people – I think one's a woman – have got out and are running to the side … There's a bloke there waving at them, calling them. Pilot's on his way to you now.'

'Okay. Keep watching. Don't do anything, let them get away. I'm going to switch off.'

'Okay.'

The pilot parked his aircraft as he had the time before, and once again opened the engine cowling and did something inside before walking over to the hangar. Cuff shrank back round the corner of the building and flattened himself against the massive door, not three feet from where the jerry cans were standing. The man's steps echoed softly off the side wall. He grunted as he picked up two cans, his breathing loud in the peace of the early hours. Another trip and all three cans and the ladder had been moved to the aircraft.

The *glob-glob-glob* of the fuel sloshing into the funnel was a distinctive sound in the silence. Cuff peered round the corner, but the pilot was up the ladder and focused on pouring, his head shrouded by his hood. In a minute he would be finished and would come straight past Cuff carrying his ladder and cans. Cuff had to move. He walked as quickly and quietly as he could across the front of the hangar to the next corner, and turned it.

The empty cans clanked together with every step the pilot took. Only two feet separated him from Cuff as he walked by, but his face was still as hidden as that of a cowled monk. A faint whiff of aviation gasoline hung in the air after he passed; he must have spilt some on his clothes.

The clanking went on for a hundred yards. Cuff could not follow over the open ground. A distant dim light from a car's open boot gave an uncertain silhouette to the figure loading it. The car drove away, and Cuff was none the wiser.

'Martin, you there? What's happening?'

'I'm following that van. The passengers got in it.'

'Don't be bloody silly, Martin. Stop now.'

'I'll just get the registration, then I'll come back.'

'Martin, stop. Leave it. The police can find that out later. Ginny will kill you if she knows what you're doing.'

Martin laughed. 'But you won't tell her, will you? I'll just get the registration, then I'll be back. Promise.'

Even though he was short, a frequent sniffer suffering from allergic rhinitis and physically weak, Martin had supported his friend in a host of crazy activities at school, some bordering on being illegal, with most stretching the boundaries of safe practice. He had thoroughly enjoyed those times, but always regretted that he never took more than a back-up role, keeping watch and holding things while Cuff, or CJ as he was then known, took all the risks. So, at last, when the opportunity to do something positive for the cause on his own merit arose, he took it. But Ginny kept a watchful eye on him these days, so he had to be careful how far he committed himself.

Now, Martin was hidden in the bushes and watching the scene through binoculars. Three people were bundled into the back of the van by two large men who quietly closed the doors on them. No features were visible, but the way one of the figures moved gave the impression she was female. The van drove off along the road without lights. Martin waited a few seconds then followed in like manner.

After a mile at a slow and cautious pace, the van's headlights came on and it built up speed. Martin kept his lights off, which meant it was damn difficult to stay on the road at the increased speed. Up to that point, he had not been able to read the number plate no matter how near he was. And even if he switched his lights on he would not be able to read it unless he got too close for comfort. His phone rang again – Cuff. He ignored it, concentrating on catching the van.

He was gaining on it, straining to see the road ahead in its headlights. The driver didn't brake, but the vehicle slowed. Its back doors suddenly filled his windscreen.

A violent swerve to the right. The hedge at the roadside rushed at him, a ditch below it. He twisted back onto the road, his car rocking with the harsh handling. He only caught a glimpse of the number as the van turned left onto a track: a single letter X, two of three digits, a 2 and a 4, but he missed the last three characters. *Christ!* His heart was pounding. He put his lights on and took his foot off the accelerator to recover. *That was bloody close, you stupid prat.*

Not far ahead, another turning led off to the left. Martin took it, drove until he found some cover and turned around to face back to the road. He switched his interior light to permanently off and stepped out. He was in a wood. The cool night air was refreshing. He pushed his door closed as silently as possible and peered around. Nothing moved. A car hooted somewhere in the distance.

He checked his watch; it was after one. Dawn was over three hours away, and the advancing cloud had stifled the moon, which was already low in the sky.

Martin set off along the track. It was so close to the one the van had taken, it was highly likely it would take him to the same place, or very close to it at least. It wasn't easy to see, and he dared not switch on his torch. There had not been rain for a week, and when he kicked one or two stones they bounced and skittered ahead of him on the dry surface. After five minutes faint voices carried up to him, but the rising breeze whisked them away, so he couldn't be sure. He crept on. The track descended a gentle slope.

A light ahead flickered through the upper branches of a tree further down the hillside. Martin stepped cautiously, aware he could easily lose his footing on the loose surface. He was straining to see where to put his feet and constantly looking up to determine where he was in relation to the light. More voices. One was angry, bullying, the other weak and protesting. Both spoke an unintelligible foreign language.

To hell with caution. I've got to find out what's going on here. He sat on the track and rested his elbows on his knees to steady the binoculars.

By two o'clock, no longer were objects a dark grey. The moon had set and left the world in complete darkness. *There's no point in sitting here any longer. I might as well leave, but I'd really like to know what's going on down there.*

The van's headlights were still on. Several torches moved about and, as they flashed in different directions, he managed to build a picture of the site. The two tracks led down to what appeared to be an old farm. There was a small house, some dilapidated sheds and a barn. The wood enclosed it completely. Sizeable trees, left to grow unhindered for decades, had almost engulfed the house.

Martin could not contain his curiosity. He was perhaps only forty yards away from the van, which was parked close to the barn door. The argument below him had stopped. A group of people had been standing between the vehicle and the barn, but as the angry talk subsided, they all went into the building, a jostling, shoving group. A few moments later, two men came out and closed and padlocked the door.

He was so absorbed he hadn't noticed, but it was now well after two. He had to go. Cuff would be worrying, and the last thing he wanted was for Ginny to be alerted if he didn't make contact soon.

Reaching some conclusion from everything he'd seen was not simple. The men had bundled and shoved those passengers into the van. There had been a one-sided argument in a foreign language before some people were pushed into the barn and the door was padlocked. From the moment they set foot on the runway, they were under someone else's control. Were the people on the flight the same ones who were now in the barn? They must be. *If they've been smuggled into Britain, then surely their countrymen should treat them as newcomers who need help, not push them around and lock them up?*

Martin got into his car and sat for a moment without starting it. His head was down, studying his phone to call Cuff. A movement caught his eye. He looked up. *Oh shit!*

Three featureless figures stood in front of the car. Each had a weapon: a heavy stick, an iron bar, a pick handle.

Martin started the engine. The men did not move. He put the car in gear and crept forward. The men didn't budge. His mind raced. He was trapped, running them down was not an option. He moved further forward slowly, giving them an opportunity to get out of the way. One of them came round to his side of the car. Another went to the passenger side. Martin watched them carefully and pressed the universal locking. As he glanced at the left one, his own window shattered in a shower of glass. The pick handle followed through and struck him on the temple. The other side window smashed inward.

Slowed for a second by the shock, Martin let the clutch out and charged forward, straight at the man in front. He didn't care – they were going to kill him. It was him or them, and his weapon was the car. The faceless bastard jumped on the bonnet. The iron bar swung down. It descended in slow motion, straight at his face. The windscreen held in place, but was suddenly a crystallised sheet of glinting ice, with a small clear patch in front of him. He put his foot down. The wheels spun on the gravel. The man on the other side had the door open. He jumped. He was in the car. He knocked it out of gear, reached across and killed the engine. Martin's head smacked back to the headrest from the next blow and blood streamed freely from his nose.

They marched him down the track to the old farm. He was sniffing. This wasn't rhinitis, this was mostly blood. They hadn't tied him, but they were bigger than he was, on either side of him and behind, and armed with those heavy clubs. He was shoved towards the barn. There was more shouting in a strange language, before another man hurried over and opened the lock. Two of them grabbed his arms with strong, hard fingers and hustled him inside and over to a stall. A length of chain appeared. It was wrapped tightly round his waist, padlocked and locked again to a post.

Martin wasn't going anywhere.

The men left taking their torches with them. Splits in the wooden walls and gaps in the roof high above revealed there was a fraction more light outside the building than in. It was not enough to make out details. As soon as he heard the barn door closing, he put his hands out in front of him and tested the range the chain would allow him to roam. He could get as far as his stall door, which was chest high, but no further. He touched the exterior wall, and the division with the next stall – both were rough and fibrous. He poked around the floor to find it was scattered with straw, then sat with his back against the post he was anchored to. The place was old and must have housed animals at one time: horses, maybe cows or sheep; but the smell of livestock had dwindled to a faint, unspecific rural odour.

He listened but heard nothing. Ginny and their future together pushed his fear into the background. Much later, the dawn chatter of birds crept into his consciousness. More light filtered through gaps in the wooden cladding of the building, and his surroundings gradually took form and added detail to his earlier views. There was a brief conversation between two men somewhere outside, but that didn't last long, and the barn's old wooden frame creaked as it resisted an early breeze. Otherwise silence.

Was that a whisper? Martin held his breath. There it was again, and another.

'*Tjeta?*' The voice was hesitant, as if it wanted to be heard, but not invite trouble.

'Hello,' Martin called, not afraid to break the silence. 'Who's there?'

'Hello. You UK?'

'Yes. Who are you?'

Martin learned there were five men there, locked in the adjacent stall. He couldn't see them, because the dividing wall was too high, maybe over six foot. There had been two women as well, but they were taken away, the man said, clearly angry. One began crying in the background when the subject was mentioned.

They had been told they were going to work in the fields, picking crops, but nothing had happened yet. They could not escape, the speaker said, because their passports and money had been taken. They came from Albania, and all they wanted was a better life in Britain. They had paid a lot of money to get here, and now this. They were prisoners and, even if they did escape, they could not go to the police.

'I can help you,' Martin said. 'They are going to make slaves of you, and you will never escape. If you can get me out of here, I can lead you to safety.'

'We don't want police. They send us home.'

A lengthy discussion went on in a half whisper, with the occasional raised voice. Martin waited.

'Hello?'

'I'm here.' *Chained here like one of the slaves these people will be.*

'Some are very frightened. Some want to go with you.'

'You must all do the same thing. If I get out of here I will tell the police where it is, and they will find you if you stay. If you come with me I can get you to a safe place and leave you. I won't tell the police. I'm chained up and cannot escape unless you can open these locks.'

More discussion. A swarthy head with tousled black hair appeared above the divider. He must have been standing on something. He peered down at Martin and saw what the problem was. The head vanished again. More hushed chattering.

The barn door opened with a creak. Light flooded the interior. Four men walked past Martin's stall to the next one. The door opened. Orders were shouted at the prisoners in what he now knew to be Albanian. Some protested and one pleaded. Two distinct thumps were followed by cries of pain.

The forced labour, compulsory labour – whatever the politically correct term was; to Martin the poor people were slaves – were shoved along the front of his stall. Two of them glanced sideways at him as they passed. One young man's eyes were red from crying. They all looked cowed.

Silence followed for some ten minutes, then a vehicle started. A bit more shouting of orders, and the van drove away. A man came back into the barn and put half a loaf of bread and a mug of water down inside the stall.

Standing on the doorstep, Cuff had that same schoolboy mixture of fear and anticipation of pain as when he was deliberately kept waiting outside the headmaster's study for a few strokes of the cane, before the practice was eventually banned. By the time he had turned fourteen, the ban was in place and the pain element had gone, but fear of the consequences would never fully go away. Today was even worse, though, because this was personal and involved his friends. The truth was he was ashamed to face Ginny. She was going to give him a bollocking second to none. He could live with that, but not with the reality that his friend and the love of her life had probably got himself into a very dangerous situation.

It was almost six o'clock in the morning. He had called several times and left messages on Martin's phone. At first it was not a concern – the silly bugger had probably forgotten to switch his ringer back on and never heard the calls. But it wasn't that, was it. No. It was much more serious – face it. Cuff drove round to where he had left his friend watching the runway and took the only route the van, with Martin following, could have driven. He found nothing. He passed three crossroads and was wasting time. They could have taken any turning or just carried on straight.

He phoned Ginny.

There was an ominous silence when he told her. 'Police. Now,' she snapped. 'I've had enough of your stupid actions. You're always putting Martin in danger.'

'I'm already on my way there, Ginny.' Cuff's voice was

subdued and quiet.

'Pick me up. I'm coming with you to see you're open with them. No more keeping things to yourself so you can try to solve them alone. I'll be ready in ten.'

He knocked on the door and Ginny opened it before he could rap it a third time. Short, red-haired, thick horn-rimmed glasses and a red jacket, she was fired up for a serious battle. She locked her door and went straight to Cuff's car without a word. The term fury didn't do her justice, and Cuff waited for her to vent it on him. But fuelling that rage was worry, a desperate concern for her man. Cuff understood entirely.

On the way to the police station, Ginny let him have it in a torrent of words that Cuff allowed to flow over him without response. She only paused once, when she dabbed at her eyes with a tissue.

He could have said he told Martin not to follow the van, that it was not his fault, that Martin was a responsible adult making his own choices, but he didn't. He accepted that he had encouraged his friend to participate, and he was sorry about that. He did argue kindly that Ginny should calm down and use her energy to help find her man rather than tear Cuff apart.

Detective Inspector Baker offered them tea. 'I'm having one.'

'Yes please,' Cuff answered.

Ginny was drumming her fingers on the desk and fidgeting. 'No thank you.'

'A person that's been missing for only a few hours does not normally warrant a search.' The DI told them. 'I'm sorry, but given what might be migrant smuggling and the theft of an aircraft, there's a real possibility your Martin is in danger from a violent gang. There's no way of telling at this stage how far he's been taken, if that is in fact what's happened. He could be nearby or on his way to Wales, London or the North for all we know. I'll put out an alert for his car and also a dark-coloured van that may contain illegals.'

Ginny handed him a photo. 'I've brought this picture of Martin. I'd like it back, please.'

'Of course. We have to consider where these allegedly illegal immigrants are going. We know the most prominent destinations, and the police in those areas will investigate. The other thing we can consider is forced labour – slavery.'

Ginny gulped audibly. The horror in her eyes was clear.

Inspector Baker looked at her without saying anything for a moment. 'Slavery is rife in the UK, believe it or not. If those illegals are going to be taken advantage of, they have to work somewhere. Agriculture often – and how do we tell the difference between a migrant worker from the EU and someone there under duress?'

It was a rhetorical question. Neither Ginny nor Cuff tried to answer.

'Don't get me wrong. It's not likely your partner will be enslaved, because they have no hold over him. With the foreigners, they'll take their passports and money so they can't run away. But let's not get ahead of ourselves with theories. We need to get forensics onto that aircraft. We need to identify the pilot and see what else we can find that might come in useful now or later.'

'I don't know how much you'll get from the Cessna, Inspector; just about every instructor in the school will have handled that machine.'

'There might be evidence from the passenger seats we can use in respect of the immigrants, if that's what they are.'

'I know what I'm going to do,' Cuff announced as they left the police station. They both had a great deal more to think about than when they went in.

12

13 August

She had left her phone on the bedside table as usual with the alarm set for six. Fed up with the three o'clock calls, Imogen had turned the ringer off, but this time she forgot to put the phone face down and it lit up, waking her. She was so angry, she lay awake for another hour. Even though they had been to the police, she was determined to bring the stalker down herself – but how? Over and over again – how?

By nine o'clock, Imogen had pulled herself together. A knock on the door startled her. In her tired and sensitive mood, fear rose. Was this him? There was no spy hole for her to see who was there. The knock came again; it was quite forceful. She turned the knob on the latch and, with her foot behind the door as a stop, opened it a crack.

'Read your electric meter, please, lady?' The voice

belonged to no one she knew. She peered round the door. A man was holding up an ID card with the supplier's logo and his name on it. He had a coarse but pleasant face which approximated the photo on the card.

'Sure, come in. Sorry, I was busy.' She was suddenly ashamed of herself. This stalking was putting her on edge, and her reaction to this innocent man was pure paranoia.

She pulled the door wider for him. A splash of bright red paint on the outside caught her eye. The spray can had lingered over the letters for too long and all of them had run. The word was at an acute angle, climbing to the right, giving emphasis to the slur – *WHORE!* The exclamation mark had dribbled from head height to the floor, leaving a single red spot at the entrance.

Imogen gasped, her hand to her mouth. The man squeezed past her, avoiding her without meeting her eye. Seeing nothing, she was vaguely aware of him entering the readings on his machine. He made a move to go, but she was standing in the doorway staring at the obscenity.

'Excuse me, please.'

She moved out of the way. 'Mmh.' Her hand was still covering her mouth.

The man avoided her look, but he didn't leave immediately. He shifted from one foot to the other then ventured, 'That's ugly, that is. Best get it off as quick as possible. Thanks. Enjoy your day.'

What a stupid mechanical thing to say! How the hell am I going to enjoy today with that there? How the hell am I going to get it off?

Instead of scrubbing off the vulgar insult – she had no thinners – Imogen found her oldest bath towel and, as an emergency measure, stuck it over the door, hammering in the pins with the heel of her shoe. While she was doing this, her mobile gonged several times with messages. She put off looking at them, knowing something upsetting was waiting for her.

Melissa wasn't on duty until later and was in the bathroom. Imogen's cry of rage and frustration had her rushing out, still wrapped in her towel. She spent some time examining the paint, and was still doing so when Imogen switched on the kettle, unlocked her phone and swore.

'What now?' Melissa asked.

Imogen crossed the room and handed over the phone. 'Each message would be too long, so they're split into two sets of three texts. What do you make of it?'

Melissa read them out loud. 'First one: *"My own gorgeous creature. Those images of you in your natural state entice me. The way you move, the way you laugh and smile engages me, draws me to you."*

'Next: *"I smell your fear at times. Do not fear me. I will not harm you, but he might. Why would I harm something I love and desire above all else?"*

'Next: *"You are mine and mine alone to love, to hold and to lay down. You will come to me. You will love me. You will lie with me."'*

Imogen pointed. 'See, the next ones are from a different number.'

'Mmh. That question again – two men, or same man, different phone?' Melissa carried on reading. '*"You have seen I mean what I say. The bike was a lesson, you have to understand I WILL punish you unless you mend your ways."*

'And: *"Do you make love with your friend? Tell her to go. You should only be with a husband not another woman. It is not natural."* That's a bit cheeky. Do you want to make love to me, Imo, darling?

'*"Finally, if you do not exhibit exemplary behaviour, I will assume your exhibitionism is a gift to the world, and the world will share your impeccable form."* Cocky bastard. He's twisted, Imo, I don't like the threat in that last one.'

'These two men are well coordinated. They must get together when they send these texts. There's very little time between nice and nasty.'

'About the same as changing the SIM card on your phone?' Melissa teased. 'If it really is two people winding you up, who do you think it might be? You say Jimmy likes to joke and make fun of people, so in this instance he's playing the adoring one and Mike is taking an ugly, vengeful stance. They get together and have a bit of fun.'

'Oh God, no! I don't believe Jimmy would do that. I told you, he's not vindictive. Mike, on the other hand, might get one of his adoring students to play the other part, the nice-guy part. That's a real possibility.'

'You've not included Cuff in this assessment. If he's involved, he has to be the nice guy. You saw that the other night.'

'I don't know what to believe any more. I'm so confused.'

'You're confusing yourself, Imo. Not least by thinking this is two men. The most realistic scenario is it's only one man creating a Dr Jekyll and Mr Hyde situation, and that man is not Cuff. He tried to catch that bloke the other night and got his face kicked in for his trouble. Surely you have to take him off your list of suspects? Nothing points in his direction except the timing of some texts he sent.'

'Maybe. I suppose so. I need to fly again. I'll have to brave it out with Cuff and hope he's innocent. It's shitty, Melissa, I can't relax or concentrate fully, and I know it will affect my flying. And this threat to make the photos public is scary. I'll have to crawl into a little hole and hide if they go onto the internet. I mean, they could stay out there for ages and even ruin my chance of getting into an airline.'

Melissa put her hand on Imogen's. 'If anyone is going to understand your problems and how they relate to flying, it'll be Cuff. I bet you he'll be supportive, even though you've been pretty mean. I'm here now. Two's safer, and we'll stick together as much as possible. We're going to clear this up – hit it straight on. We confronted Cuff, and he proved to us it's not him. You think it's Mike? We can do the same with him. If it is him and he doesn't give up, we'll take him to the police.'

'No. I'm not talking to Mike. He's not like Cuff, he'll get aggressive and even more obnoxious. He'll just lie his way out of it, so we'll get nowhere.'

'Not another one,' Imogen said as her phone tolled its message tone. '*"I need to shop 4 food pick me up after 4 then i'll have a couple of beers at u place any in the fridge mel should get lost unless she want to join in."*'

'Bastard! I'm sick of this fucking man. He's compounding my problems. How the hell did I ever let him into my life? Aagh!' She hurled the phone across the room. It hit the wingback chair, bounced and dropped to the carpet.

First thing on Wednesday morning, Sonia entered the crew room and spotted Mike at the coffee machine. Without a greeting she asked him when he was going to be fit enough to fly again. 'It's putting a strain on the others with you out of action.'

'Should only be another week, the doc says. What the fuck's it got to do with yah?'

However Sonia addressed Mike, whether it was with contempt, scorn or impatience, he never seemed to notice, which frustrated her. 'Everything. I'm running this operation.'

Mike didn't answer, but when she reached the door of Connor's office she looked back. He was staring at her, open mouthed. A reaction at last. He appeared to pull himself together and limped after her. He had stopped using crutches, but still had his boot on. He closed the door behind him and crossed over to the desk. Sonia turned her back to the room and looked out of the window towards the runway.

'You can leave that open, it's warming up already.' Connor's drooping eyes portrayed a lack of sleep.

'This is confidential,' Mike replied, and left the door as it was. 'What's going on? Sonia says she's running the operation.'

'I am,' she said to what she hoped was the last shower before it cleared. She turned back to face the two men with her arms folded and her chin up.

'I've given her that responsibility. What have you got there?' The weakness in Connor's tone matched his appearance. He sounded as if he was trying to be pleasant as he leaned across his desk with an expression which was more questioning than his trademark hint of disapproval or distaste.

'The technical log and some of the maintenance records for the Cessna 172.' Mike dumped them on the desk and pushed them towards Connor.

'Why?'

'It's only flown a few hours since the last inspection, so I drew the records from the previous one. Compare the engine tachometer reading to the Hobbs time.'

Connor picked up the books but didn't open them. Instead he replaced them on the desk in precise alignment with the edge.

Sonia left the window and crossed to the desk. She took the books from Connor and opened them. 'You know perfectly well, the tachometer time is always exceeded by the Hobbs time, because it's not measuring time, it's actually measuring engine revolutions above a certain level, but not at idle, whereas the Hobbs runs as soon as the engine starts.'

'Yeah, of course I know that, but this tacho gained on the Hobbs by about ten hours. That means the Hobbs has been switched off for that time. The tech log is the same as the

Hobbs time, so someone's been using the machine and not recording it.'

Connor leaned back and folded his arms. 'You look as if you have more to tell me – us?'

Mike sat. 'Yeah, I do.'

The news of Sonia's promotion, as everyone thought of it, spread quickly through the school. They all congratulated her, and every instructor except Mike said it was about time. Her morale was already high with her accomplishment, but the community's reaction gave it an extra boost.

Humming softly to herself, she entered Connor's office to find he was not having a good day. She knew why, of course. He'd been robbed of his responsibility for the school, and that odious Mike Penny's discovery must be weighing him down as well. It was serious, but she was confident enough to deal with it, whereas Connor looked defeated.

He held the telephone receiver to his ear, but it appeared the call was over. Other than an initial flicker of a glance, he couldn't look at her and kept his face down or stared vacantly out of the window.

He couldn't address her by name either. 'You'd better know what's happened. Someone's reported that the Cessna 172 has been used for illegal night flights, probably smuggling. We'll have to take it out of the programme until further notice. The police are going to examine it for clues. They'll be here in half an hour. This is a disaster. We don't need this kind of publicity. I hope to God the press don't get hold of it.'

'How do the police know about it?'

'I don't know, they only said a source told them.'

Detective Inspector Baker introduced himself and informed Sonia and Connor that he wanted full access to the Cessna and to talk to all the instructors. He asked if any of the students had the ability to conduct night flights to France and land on an unlit runway. Sonia told him there were none, although one or two might have thought they could.

The news that the police had isolated the 172 with tape and were crawling all over it flew round the school like a gust of wind. There was nothing they could do to ease the situation and Sonia took it in her stride. She had a frisson of schadenfreude over Connor's enhanced misery, as his carefully organised flying programme dissolved into chaos.

With students waiting to fly and instructors waiting to be interviewed, the crowd in the crew room became far too big. Sonia listened to the wild, speculative theories being expressed. How could people come up with such rubbish when they knew nothing?

A group of students had gathered by their idol. 'What's going on, Mike, do you know?'

'Yeah, but I can't say anything right now. It's pretty sensitive. I'll let yah know when it's okay to do so.'

Sonia gave a mental eye roll and shook her head.

Connor became more and more bad tempered through the day and picked on people, both students and instructors. To all of them he said, 'If anyone breathes a word of this to the press, they can find another school,' and to individuals, 'Pick that up. For God's sake keep this place tidy,' along with, 'Whose coffee mug is this left lying here?' and 'Why haven't these manuals been put back in the library?'

'Connor!' Sonia beckoned from his office.

He followed her in, glanced briefly at her and looked to the side.

'Connor, these people are our customers, our students. They are not airmen you can pull rank on. Are you trying to drive them away?'

'We can't afford bad publicity. I don't want them going to

the press.'

'You're not going to achieve that by losing your self-control.'

'Humph!'

Cuff had not seen Imogen since they tried to catch the stalker, and that was almost two weeks ago. It was surprising, given her enthusiasm for flying.

She walked into the crew room with a grim face. Cuff was in The Chair and in the middle of a conversation on his phone. He was just back from talking to the police and having his ear bashed by Ginny. Imogen stopped and looked down at him, waiting for his call to finish. Cuff stood, still listening, and signalled her to take the chair.

'No thanks.'

He eventually put his phone away and said cheerfully, 'Imogen, how are you doing? I wondered if you were looking for another school to get away from the stalker. Are you back to fly?'

'Yes. I was working for my author, actually. When can I start?' Her phone pinged its message sound in her pocket. She ignored it. 'I'm not in the best of moods, I'm afraid. That bastard vandalised my front door and sent more texts last night.'

'Oh God.'

She had still not apologised for accusing him of being the stalker, but this affair must be having a greater effect on her than she showed. Allowances had to be made. 'I hope you've crossed me off your list of suspects.'

She nodded in response.

Why wasn't she prepared to admit she was wrong? This was going to take careful handling. 'I need a favour, please. I'll give you a free lesson,' Cuff offered. 'I'll pay for the whole flight. You'll fly, but I have to try and find something.'

'Why, what's going on?'

What to say to that inevitable question? 'I need to search for a stolen car. Can we leave it at that?'

'I suppose so. If you want. It's just that I could help you look if you tell me more about it.'

'I want you to fly the aircraft, not be distracted by things outside. That's the way accidents happen. We'll go this afternoon if that's okay with you? Our aircraft is not available so we'll have to take the other Cessna. Unfortunately it's having a scheduled inspection, so we can't go until after five.' His watch read ten past eleven.

Cuff walked away to get a coffee. Imogen didn't follow him; she was still standing in the middle of the room. Mike Penny was looking out from behind the closed door of a briefing room, and Connor appeared to be watching her from his office. All three of them staring at her, as if she were a caged animal. *There's something wrong here: I'm looking at her with some sympathy. Mike is angry; and Connor? Is he angry too, perhaps because she disrupted his programming with silly female notions?*

Imogen pulled her phone out. She walked over to Cuff and showed it to him. *'Have you thought about the release of the photos? I will call you. Think carefully.'*

'This comes from the number he uses for threats, not compliments. I'm getting scared. No, not scared so much as worried. Those photos being made available to the world could wreck my future!'

'That's stretching a point. They'll be long forgotten by the time you're ready to apply for a job. I didn't send that, you know.'

'I know you didn't, you were standing here.'

Cuff looked up again. Mike was hobbling through the front door towards a waiting taxi. Round to the right, Connor was looking straight at him through his window. But it wasn't certain whether the man was focused or merely staring vacantly, his mind on other things.

Another message sounded. '*Imo baby i left my stuff at the office u take it home i'll pick it up later and we can make up usual fun stuff what u say.*' Cuff pretended not to see it and handed the phone back to her.

Imogen blushed deeply. 'An emphatic NO, you bastard. I will *not* have you ordering me around. I am *not* your property. Collect your own fucking stuff.'

Cuff put out a comforting hand, but immediately dropped it – too familiar. In one way her scarlet cheeks were amusing, in another she deserved a lot of sympathy for the pressures she was under.

'So the stalker will call you? I've an idea of how we can trap this guy.'

Imogen turned the ringer off and put the phone away. 'You said 'we'; are you going to help? Why would you? What's your idea?'

'Of course I'll help, and it's because I can't resist getting involved. It's a problem I have. And of course you need help outside of the police.' The commitment had come out freely, without any spurring from his alter ego – that was good. 'Let me think it through. Right now I need to find this car, it's more important.'

Imogen stared at him. 'I don't understand – don't you think I'm under threat?'

'Oh, I'm sorry, that came across badly. Yes, of course you're threatened, but there's no sign you're in imminent danger. It could be months or longer before something drastic happens.'

'It could also be tonight. You have no way of knowing.'

'Nothing is going to happen to you in the immediate future.'

'You do not know that unless you're a part of this. I'm not budging until you explain why a car is more important than me.'

'Come outside.'

Cuff ushered Imogen to the lawn which bordered the front of the school building. 'Sit here.' He indicated one of the two picnic tables, waited until she was settled then perched on the end of the bench. 'This is highly confidential at the moment, please.'

Her eyes were accusing. They would stay angry until she got a satisfactory explanation, but she nodded her agreement.

She didn't interrupt his story, but when he'd finished she said, 'If you'd told me that in the first place, I would have fully understood. It isn't nice to not be trusted.'

'Then you know how I felt when you accused me of being the stalker.'

She gave a wan smile. 'Touché. Sorry.'

They left in a smaller Cessna 150 at a little after five thirty that afternoon with some two and a half hours of daylight remaining. He told her he believed the car was not far away, but didn't say any more about Martin being in danger.

The car had to be on a road or track, or now hidden in a barn or shed. It could be under trees. Should he use a conventional parallel search, going up and down in legs which progressively crept in one direction, or should he follow all roads and tracks and check out possible hiding places? He reckoned the creeping parallel search would waste a lot of time as much of it would be over ground which could never be used to hide the car, so he should take the second option instead.

Cuff pointed to a spot near the runway's end. 'This is where he was when I last spoke to him. Let's follow the road north and look at any tracks going off to the side. As we go, I'll mark them off on the map.'

'Okay.'

They had been airborne for over two hours. Their fuel would last until after dark, so that wasn't a problem. Cuff told her to follow a track to see where it went. It was Imogen who spotted the buildings first. They were old and almost hidden amongst trees.

'Circle it.'

It appeared to be abandoned. He caught her looking across him at the farm.

'What's your speed?'

'Er …' She glanced back to the instrument. 'Seventy.'

'You had to look for it. Fly the aircraft, Imogen – I'll do the search or we'll stall.'

'Yes, sorry,' she answered, chastened.

There was nothing worthwhile to be seen at the farm.

The girls were in their customary places in the flat. It was funny how once they had adopted these positions they always returned to them without discussion. Melissa was horizontal on the couch. Imogen usually sat in her wingback chair, but had taken to frequently and cautiously peering out of the window. 'He hasn't been back since we chased him off.'

'He'll change tactics somehow. How did it go with Cuff today?'

Imogen told her.

'How do you feel about him? Do you trust him now?'

'I don't know. I feel bad about him in a way, but I don't know what to do. He is, or rather was, definitely interested in me, but I don't want to encourage him as I really don't want another man for a while. If I think carefully—'

'Which you obviously have done.'

'—I have no reason to dislike him; but I'm scared. He's too close. No he's not, but I worry that he could be.'

'Stop putting off the inevitable, Imo. Let it go, relax and live your life.'

'You should stop interfering and trying to influence me.'
'I tried to rid you of Mike, and that was justified, wasn't it?'

13

14 August

Imogen was wearing one of her favourite black-and-white patterned tops over a pair of black jeans for their next flight. Cuff followed her into the lecture room. *She's such a pretty girl – attractive in every way, and a strong character, too. She's distracting, but she's not the main cause right now.*

Cuff 's delivery of the preflight briefing was weak. Martin was missing: he might be a captive, injured, dead – or facing it. Ginny had made it very plain she held Cuff responsible, even if it was only partially true. Ginny was a super person, and she would be severely damaged if Martin came to any harm.

Cuff's lack of focus was annoying Imogen.

'I'm sorry, I've an awful lot on my mind at the moment.'

'I know. Are you okay to fly?'

'Yes. Yes, we must.'

They took the Cessna out into the flying training area and over where they had searched the previous evening. They spent the best part of an hour on the exercises they had briefed, before Cuff declared they should go home. He waited until a suitable field for a forced landing – one not easy to reach – came into view. He pulled the throttle back to idle.

Imogen reacted by the book. Out loud she went through her immediate emergency actions for engine failure. She put the nose down to maintain speed and pointed. 'The wind's on our right, I'm going for that field there.'

Cuff sat back to observe her efforts. She was going to make the field without a problem. She was doing well: precise, controlled and not flustered like some other students. They were getting low, and there was a wood beneath them.

Every time he practised engine failures and ended in similar situations, the image of the trees rushing up to meet him during his accident recurred. They were here again now, the trees not on the hillside and level with him when he crashed, but just off the wing tip and below them.

'You'll make it easily. Nicely judged, Imogen. Go around.'

In simulated failure, the engine was ticking over, the propeller noticeably slow in the idle. Imogen opened the throttle. The engine coughed, spluttered and died. The propeller stopped at an angle off the vertical, the silence immediate.

'Continue to land! I'll try and get it started.' Cuff turned the key. The propeller hesitated through a full turn and stopped. 'No good. Too late. Focus on the landing.'

'Fuel off.'

'Good. Watch your speed, the stationary prop is extra drag. It's slowing us.'

She lowered the nose to keep the speed. The glide angle changed. The field was still there, but they were only just going to make it. A hundred feet to go. Imogen's head was thrust forward, her bottom lip imprisoned by her front teeth, her eyes flicking to the airspeed and back to her landing target.

She never looked at him. 'Don't you want to take it?'

'You've got control, Imogen. Land it!'

'It could be rough.'

'Land it!' But Cuff's feet hovered over the rudder pedals, and his hands were very close to the control yoke.

She was going to have to flare for the landing in a few seconds. Height perception was not the same as on a hard-surface runway – different judgement was required. Would she do it without being prompted? She must make the decisions.

'I'm flaring.'

Despite her obvious nerves and the white-knuckle tension in her hands, it was a smooth and gentle movement. The Cessna settled and touched. A shudder went through the airframe. The ground was uneven and rough. Tufts of grass and depressions from a hundred grazing hooves bounced the little aeroplane as it charged its way across the field, rocking them in their seats before it finally bumped to a stop.

Imogen checked that the fuel and the ignition were switched off and sat back, breathing deeply and staring ahead at what remained of the field before they would have hit a line of trees. There wasn't much.

Cuff grinned at her. 'Well done, very well handled.'

'I was petrified.'

'Rubbish, you kept your head and did an excellent job.'

'Why didn't you take it? I might have fluffed it.'

'Because it was a golden opportunity for you to prove yourself – and you did. I suppose we should tell someone we want to be rescued.' He got out and looked at his phone. 'I don't have a signal, do you?'

Imogen came round to his side of the aircraft. 'I left my phone in my locker. Sorry.'

They tried to call other aeroplanes on the radio, but from the ground it wasn't successful; maybe none were flying.

'Let's take a walk over to the house we saw from the air, the one in the wood. They should have a phone, or maybe we'll get a signal there.'

They negotiated a barbed wire fence before entering the trees. Cuff vaulted it and then used a hand and a foot to hold the wires apart for Imogen to squeeze through. He put a hand on her back to prevent her shirt catching, and removed it as soon as she was clear.

A few minutes later they found a track heading down the gentle slope to the left. It led to a clearing with the house at the far end. To the right and under some tall trees was a barn.

The door to the house had once been white, but was now a dirty cream and the paint was peeling off in strips, exposing weathered grey wood beneath. The walls were brick, but the mortar was crumbling, leaving long gaps between the courses, and in some places the bricks themselves had shed chunks. The windows were covered in grime and green mould, and nothing could be seen through the one next to the door.

Imogen knocked and stood back. 'It looks pretty run-down, do you think it's occupied?' She knocked again.

Cuff peered around the side of the house. 'There may be no one home, but there are recent tyre tracks here.'

Imogen joined him. 'More than one car.'

'Let's take a look at the barn. I still don't have a signal, but there might be one over there, you never know.'

The barn door was padlocked, and the lock appeared new. Cuff bent to examine it, when there was a sound of someone spitting behind them.

'What you want? Here private.' A short, stocky man stood

there dressed in a greasy, dark jacket over a black T-shirt, stained blue jeans and heavy boots. Narrow black eyes were pinpoints glaring out of a swarthy complexion, two days of stubble, and his thick hair was tied in a long ponytail. His feet were placed wide apart, and his double-barrelled shotgun tracked from Cuff to Imogen and back. A large German Shepherd stood beside him, panting gently, a frothy string of drool hanging from its left lip. Its hazel eyes were intense, its ears upright, forward and alert. The animal was poised, waiting for a command.

This wasn't the first time Cuff had faced an armed man. The cliff edge had been at his back when Barry Castle came at him with his long knife, but that did not make this situation any easier. Castle had to get close to use his knife, whereas this man could shoot from yards away, and the dog could leap the gap in a second.

Imogen was close beside him, remaining very still.

Cuff held his hands up level with his chest, palms outwards. 'We're sorry, we didn't mean to intrude. We need to use a telephone. Do you have one, please?'

The man shook his head once and gestured with his shotgun for them to go away. Cuff led the way up the track they had come down.

'The skin on my back is crawling,' Imogen said. 'What's the range of a shotgun?'

'Depends on a lot of things, whether it's choked, size of shot … Every step makes it less effective, keep going.'

Cuff looked back; the buildings were out of sight. 'Are you okay?'

'Yes, I'm fine. He was a bit scary, though.'

'He's not English. I wonder where he's from. And why is he so protective of that dump? We need to get in contact with the airfield. We should be back by now and they'll be worrying. It's getting late for a search tonight. Hang on, what's that through there?' Cuff pointed into the wood.

'It's a car.'

He ran forward. The wreck was burned out, and could have been any ordinary family car without the trim and the badges. It sat on the wheel rims, the tyres each having disintegrated into a brush of the steel wire belting. He walked around it trying to work out what it was. At the right rear was a large dent.

'This is Martin's car! It's the one I've been looking for. Bloody hell! What's happened to him? I've got to call the police, and we must let the school know we're safe, they'll be organising a search and rescue soon. Damn! Still no bloody signal. There must be one up near the road, surely. Come on, let's go.'

It was half past eight; the sun had set. Twilight would linger for another half hour, but it was becoming difficult to pick out detail in the woods either side of the track.

'*Stop*. Listen: there's a car coming.' Imogen pulled at his sleeve.

'Back into the trees, quick.'

Headlights darted between the trunks, flicking up and down as a black van bumped along the lane. From the shelter of a holly bush they watched it pass.

What to do? Take a risk, go down to the farm and send Imogen for help; or take the safest choice, which was for both of them to carry on to the road and get hold of the police? But that would leave Martin a prisoner for even longer, and who knew what threat he was facing, if indeed he was even there. *What would 'Jonathan' do?*

'Stay here, Imogen. I'm going back there to see what's going on. I've got a weird feeling about this place. Something isn't right.'

'I know. That foreign man and his gun, the new lock on the

barn. What was he trying to protect? But I'm coming with you.'

'No—'

'No *nos* about it. I'm not being left here on my own, and I may be able to help.'

'Listen to me, Imogen. Martin may be held down there by some very dangerous people. Those night flights involved either drugs or people-smuggling. Whichever, the gangs who do that kind of thing think nothing of killing. I have to find out where Martin is. I'm partly responsible for him being missing. You have nothing to do with this. This is not your battle, and I'm not having another innocent person involved. Please, go to the main road, flag down a car and get the hell out of here. You'll only be a hindrance.'

'A *hindrance*. Bloody cheek. And I resent being classed as a helpless female as well.'

'I didn't—'

'You implied it. I'm just as good as you are; not physically, but every other way. I owe you for becoming involved with the stalker anyway. I don't want any debt to *you* hanging over me.'

'You don't owe me anything. I tried to catch him out of common decency.'

'I'm coming, and you can't stop me unless you force me to stay here. Are you going to force me?'

'Don't be daft, of course not.' Time and freedom to act with no distractions were going to be vital when at the farm; but short of tying her up, he couldn't stop her coming with him. Yes, she was going to be a hindrance, though.

'If you have to come, then don't argue about anything I say. There might be a time when we have to do something quickly, and a discussion about that could be the end of us. We can save arguments for later.'

They trotted down the track after the van and reached a

place where they could see the front of the barn. The vehicle was parked, and the rear doors were open. Some men were getting out as Imogen and Cuff stopped and sat on the road to get the best view through the vegetation. Three other big, solid men were standing near the barn's door, effectively stopping the passengers from going anywhere other than into the building. Where was Martin? A smaller man, his shotgun still in his hands, was standing to one side and staring up the hill in their direction, his dog beside him. Cuff told himself they would not be seen in the dimming light, unless …

Imogen moved.

'Keep absolutely still,' Cuff whispered.

The stocky man turned his head towards one of the others and vanished round the side of the building, his dog at his heels. The guard left the group and followed him. The prisoners had all been hustled into the barn by the other two guards.

'I want to take a closer look. Something's not right about this. It looks like forced labour to me. Stay here in case you have to go for help.'

Imogen opened her mouth to argue. A twig snapped in the semi-darkness to their left. Cuff turned in that direction, and Imogen glanced at him. He grabbed her hand and pulled her to her feet. 'Let's get out of here.'

They walked away at first, then ran. Cuff looked back. An indistinct shape, a movement. 'Into the wood!' he panted and led her off to the right. The forest darkness enveloped them. Dim light filtered through the canopy, but it would not last long. The moon, two days from full, had risen an hour ago, but was still too low to penetrate the trees. Already, unseen fallen branches forced them into slow progress or be tripped. An occasional crunch of leaves, the crack of breaking twigs, the rustle of a bush as it caught a sleeve – the sounds were getting closer. If they could hear their hunters, then the men could hear them too, and the dog certainly could. But noise was unavoidable unless they stopped moving.

A fallen tree, a large silver birch downed in a high wind, lay across their path. Its pale bark drew attention as an almost luminous barrier to progress. Beyond it lay another trunk, much thicker and heavier, perhaps a type of poplar. It had been uprooted much earlier than the birch, and new shoots, fed by roots which still clung to the soil, sprouted vertically from its horizontal trunk. Cuff pulled Imogen down and pushed her beneath it. He followed, worming his way further under the tree until they lay, top of head to top of head, in the damp earth and were almost completely hidden.

Almost. 'Damn! My white shirt.'

Imogen was quick. She left her refuge and crouched next to him, throwing leaves and mud over him as best she could.

'No time for more, get back under here,' he hissed.

Her head was against his in the confines of their hide, and it was warming. Her perfume had not faded during the day. Spicy, a hint of smokiness maybe? It was seductive, and the desire to pull her even closer was strong. Was it only because he had not had romantic feelings for a woman for almost two years, or was it because he was attracted to her in particular? No matter, this was certainly not the time nor the place; and in any case, she had expressed no interest in him at all.

Suppressed by their cover, the sounds of pursuit were dim. There was no way of knowing if the men had stopped and were listening, or had missed them and gone away. Imogen made to move. Cuff felt her stir and reached over his shoulder to keep her still. Nearby, another snap of breaking wood. Don't breathe. A rapid panting was close, much too close.

From ground level, the view crossed a carpet of thousands of dead leaves. The German Shepherd was only a few yards away; the silhouette of its distinctive upright ears stood out against the silver bark of the dead birch. The dog was straining in their direction. It was interested, it knew they were there, but their scent was not what it had been trained to look for; it was not the smell of unwashed, enslaved bodies and dirty, sweat-soaked clothing. It wanted to investigate, but it wasn't moving. It must be leashed. A faint sound of crashing undergrowth came from much further away, followed by a brief exchange of whispers between two men close by.

Some excited activity was happening at the farm: screams and shouts, along with other noises which, although they gave no clue, weren't normal. Then silence for a while. Calls from the farm were answered by their pursuers, who spoke urgently to each other making little effort to be quiet. It was too dark for Cuff to see beyond the dog, but the animal was pulled away by a larger shadow.

They waited in silence until Cuff carefully lowered his hand from Imogen's head and checked his watch – a quarter past nine. In the distance, an engine struggled into life after half a dozen grinding turns of the starter. Angry shouts. Doors slammed, and the engine noise increased. Cuff checked his watch again, even though only a few moments had passed. They had been hidden for over half an hour and there had been no hint of pursuit since the dog had picked up their scent.

'Okay, let's go, but keep it quiet. It sounds like they've gone, but they may be waiting for us to move.'

'I've lost direction,' Imogen whispered. 'Which way?'

'It's uphill to the road. I'll bet those men were enslaved. Martin was following a dark van with illegals in it and he never returned. I'll also bet he's a prisoner there. I have to go and see.'

'All right, let's go.'

'No, Imogen, don't start that again. This is dangerous, and it's not your fight. Please go to the main road and wait for me there.'

'You want me to walk through these woods alone with those thugs roaming around looking for me? I'm safer with you.'

Argument was clearly futile, and time could not be wasted. 'Come on then, let's go.'

14

14 August – Late

Martin's hours were long. He had explored every possibility of escape. The barn's exterior wooden walls were rotting, and could be broken out without too much effort –were it not for his chain. Climbing up to the roof and squeezing through one of the holes open to the sky might be possible – were it not for his chain.

The previous afternoon a light aircraft had flown low overhead and appeared to circle before the noise of its engine faded into the distance. Was that Cuff searching for him?

It was after eight thirty before the van returned and the prisoners were herded back into their stall. It would be dark soon.

'Hello?'

'I'm here,' Martin replied.

Some scrabbling sounds and a few grunts preceded a head peering over the top of the dividing wall. 'I think maybe they kill you. They talking. One say you must die, another say that stupid, dangerous. Better they hide you. Give them time, then they leave here and change business. I not know what they decide.'

'Nice! Can you help me get out of here? Then I can help you.'

'Bardhyl say the lock easy. He get wire today, he try. He come now.' The head vanished. Another head appeared, white teeth bright in the dim light.

Bardhyl jumped down into the straw. He had some in his filthy hair and on his jacket. He produced a piece of wire, dropped to his knees and studied the padlock. The stink of unwashed labour rose to Martin's nostrils.

Bardhyl gripped the end of the wire in his teeth and bent it into a tiny right angle before straightening out the rest. He showed Martin how flexible the wire was and shrugged his shoulders as if to express his doubt that it was strong enough. He fiddled and worried at the padlock for a while, his face contorted with concentration, until he eventually shook his head.

Bloody hell, I'm in trouble. He pointed to the other lock on the post end of the chain. Bardhyl nodded and crawled across the floor.

Martin could no longer see what the Albanian was doing. Things were getting really scary. Would they come for him tonight? The bread and water at breakfast was long gone. But worse than the hunger was that they would not bother to waste food on a condemned man.

Bardhyl turned to him with a grim expression. He again showed Martin how flexible the wire was. He shook his head and shrugged his shoulders in a hopeless gesture. He shoved the post, but there was no give in it.

Martin stared up to the top of the pole, trying to make out detail. It was not joined to the rafter above, as he had first thought, but was well out of reach for one man. He took Bardhyl by the shoulders, pushed him back against the post and indicated with hand signals what he wanted him to do.

Bardhyl grinned at the new idea and cupped his hands into a step. Martin clambered up to stand on the Albanian's shoulders, pulling the loop of chain that was round the pillar up with him. He still could not reach high enough; he was a foot short. He tried to flick the loop over the top. It jammed every time.

Bardhyl put his hands under Martin's feet, held him where he was and turned around to face the post. Martin clung to the wood and tried to climb. It was hopeless. Then his feet were firmly pushed upwards as Bardhyl straightened his arms and lifted him higher. *I wish I had such strength.*

The loop passed over the top at the first try. Bardhyl lowered Martin to the floor, smiling broadly at his success.

Martin clasped the Albanian's arm and shook his hand. He indicated that the man should get back over onto his own side of the division. He cupped his hands together for him to use as a step to reach the top, but Bardhyl shook his head and led the way out into the central passage.

The Albanians were held in what might have been a storeroom. The walls were higher than the animal stalls, and the door was bolted closed, but not locked. It was the main barn door which trapped them all.

Martin was still chained around his waist and had almost three yards of loose metal to carry. He draped it over his shoulder a couple of times and held the free end in his right hand. He stood in the doorway of the storeroom. Like Bardhyl, the prisoners were dishevelled, dirty and stank. *When did these poor buggers last have a chance to wash? They're scruffy, but there's more about them than that. It's the look of defeat on their faces. They've overcome who knows what in the way of obstacles to get to Britain, have paid what to them must have been vast sums to traffickers to assist their passage, only to be beaten up and enslaved on arrival. And there's only one reason their women have been separated from them. That young man with red-rimmed eyes, he was the one who had been sobbing over the love of his life. Poor girl has probably been forced into whoredom already.*

If they were going to get out of this, they had to be galvanised into action. Martin repeated his arguments of the day before: 'Help me get out of here, and I will get you to a safe place, give you a little money and leave you alone. I will not tell the police anything except how to find these men who are using you. I must tell them that.'

'Police find us. Send back.' This sounded as if it was said by the same man who had spoken to him originally.

'Which is better, to go home or work for these people for the rest of your life? Bad food, locked up, no future. If I tell the police, at least they might find your women and save them. I'm sure they would prefer to go home rather than be prostitutes.'

The men huddled together and talked in hushed tones with the exceptional angry outburst from one of them, frustrated at the others' lack of understanding. 'You go, we stay.'

Martin sighed. He no longer needed them to help him escape; Bardhyl had already freed him, but he couldn't bear to see them accepting a life of slavery so easily. *Why can't they see there's only one option?*

'When I get out I'm going to the police to have these men arrested. The police will find you then. If you help me get out and come with me, you have a chance to be free and make a life.'

They went back to mumbling between themselves.

Come on. Make up your minds. Every moment you dither brings the end of my life that much closer!

Eventually, it appeared the group had reached consensus over something. Did that mean a general agreement on what to do had been reached? Had they got the message at last?

'I must go now. They may come to kill me anytime. Are you coming with me or not?'

More muttering. 'We come.'

'This is an old barn, it looks rotten, it must be weak somewhere. We need to find a place to make a hole we can get through.'

Bardhyl alone was an optimistic type. Before Martin had finished speaking he started looking around. The others, as if suddenly realising they were part of this, that they could be free if they tried, joined in the search. Someone found a rotten section and kicked it out. Bardhyl led the way, on his belly, worming his way between the cladding and the ground. His jacket caught; someone freed him. Suddenly they were all fidgeting to get into the gap – impatient to be out.

'Are you ready to fight?' Martin said.

'Fight?'

'Get angry. These men have robbed you of freedom and taken your women. Get very angry.'

The translation caused nods and murmurs. A couple of them flexed their arms.

Twilight had begun, and the air was cooler than inside the barn. The last prisoner emerged from the hole. They gathered together and all looked at Martin – which way?

No way. Three big men, each with his iron bar, heavy stick or pick handle, stood watching them, waiting.

Martin was used to bullies, but they were never armed like this. 'Three of them, six of us,' he yelled at the immigrants, and advanced a step. The man facing him was raising his eyebrows repeatedly, egging Martin on to be beaten. He hefted his iron bar from one hand to the other, defying Martin to come closer.

The Albanians did not move. Martin took another step. 'Come on, back me up! We *must* fight them.'

The young man with the red, tearful eyes, the slim youth who had lost his love, broke from the group and took two strides. Pick-man put both hands on the shaft of his weapon and raised it across his chest, ready. The others, shamed by their young friend, shifted forward.

With lightning speed, the youth pivoted on one foot, spun a full turn and fired a taekwondo head-high kick. The boy radiated hatred. It gave immense power to that kick. These men had taken this lad's girl and maybe even shared her amongst themselves before selling her on.

The thug staggered and dropped to his knees. The illegals were inspired and charged forward. Bardhyl roared. The interpreter screamed, his teeth bared.

Iron-rod waited for Martin, grinning. Martin had never been a fighter. He didn't look one – he was too small, too weedy. But he had a weapon. There was nothing to lose with his life at stake. This man would kill him with that bar. He would kill him if he turned and ran. The only option was to fight. He unwound one loop of the chain from his shoulder, so he now had a good length in his right hand. He whirled it round his head and advanced, clearing a six-foot arc.

Iron-rod pushed his weapon forward to catch the chain. It did and spun itself round the bar. Martin pulled. The man was too big and heavy to move, but he was caught off balance. Martin did the only other thing he could think of – he kicked and connected. Iron-rod yelped and doubled over, dropping his bar with the chain still wound on it.

One of the Albanians grabbed the weapon and swung it down on the slaver, and again, and again, until he lay still. Two other captives had managed to drop the third man and were beating him with his own stick.

'Stop,' Martin yelled at the interpreter. 'Tell them to stop, they must not kill them. Come, we must go.'

Martin led the group up the track he had come in on. Going through the wood was an option, but what if he muddled the direction and they got lost? There might be a chance the thugs had left his keys in his car, and all six of them could make their escape. But that hope was soon dashed. The old machine had been torched. It stank of burned plastic and paint. The steering wheel was nothing but a metal ring, and springs were all that were left within the seat frames.

Will the insurance fork out for this? Forget it, there are more important issues right now. An engine revved behind them. Martin rushed the Albanians into the wood to hide. They needed no encouragement.

The black van came up the hill and carried on past the car. In a few moments it would be at the tarred road, but it stopped. Martin waited, listening. Shouting from the direction of the van was answered from the woods on their right. Voices at a normal level came from the van, but they were angry and an argument ensued. Had all the men come out of the wood and gathered there?

The van's engine came to life. A moment later doors were slammed, and it drove away. The note died briefly before it accelerated into the distance. It must have reached the road.

'I think they've gone, escaped before the police come.'

'You tell police?'

'Yes, but not before you are safe. I mean, those men may think we will go to the police immediately, and this place will be searched, but I will do that later. Don't worry – if they have gone and won't be coming back, you can stay the night back in the barn. I will go home and come back early tomorrow with help. Where will you go? Do you have an address where there is safety?'

There was some muttering and a grubby scrap of paper was produced. It was too dark to read, so Martin stuffed it in his pocket.

He sent the group back to the barn before climbing up to the road. How far was the airfield from here – five miles? No phone, no money and no watch: the slavers had taken them all. His only possession was a chain locked round his waist with three yards of the heavy metal wound over his shoulder. It was a cool evening. To stop would invite cold – keep moving.

A car was coming. He stuck out his thumb. It ignored him and carried on. Five more cars passed without stopping. In the 'good old days', he'd been told, drivers would give a hiker a lift without a qualm. But in the current world trust had gone; people were wary of strangers, or everyone was in such a great hurry they didn't have time to stop.

Martin reached the edge of the airfield at last, the place from where he had watched the Cessna land. He looked for lights in Cuff's flying school on the far side, but everyone had gone home. He walked on. Ginny was waiting, her welcoming clutches spurring him to a quicker pace.

15

14, 15 August

There was no sound from the barn. The door was still padlocked, but Imogen had found a hole in the side wall at ground level. Cuff crawled inside and Imogen followed. He recoiled at the smell of human excrement and pointed to the stinking bucket just visible in the corner of the storeroom.

'People have been in here. They must have been prisoners.'

In the next compartment was another bucket and an empty water bottle. The rest of the barn was as normal as a barn was likely to be.

'We saw them put in, and there's no one here now. They must have escaped through that hole or been taken away. Let's go.'

The growl was deep and threatening. Cuff turned slowly and with care. The same German Shepherd, the same man, the same shotgun. Another man, much bigger and heavier, was behind the dog. He gave them a contemptuous look for a moment, made some comment and left the barn.

Cuff held Dog-man's glare. It never wavered, neither did the gun. Imogen stepped closer to him and gripped his sleeve. For an age no one moved. The only sound was the panting of the dog. Its stare was permanent and penetrating.

The heavy man returned with a coil of rope. Dog-man beckoned to Imogen. She stayed where she was. The gun was raised to her face. She obeyed, and took two strides. Cuff couldn't take his eyes off the shotgun, inches from her head, as his hands were yanked behind his back and lashed together.

Big-man did the same to Imogen.

Cuff winced as the gun was rammed into his back. They were pushed into a stall. The door was slammed and bolted. A moment later the sound of the barn door closing reached them.

Cuff tried to see her face. 'Are you okay?'

'Yes, scared to death, but okay. Are you?'

'Mmmh. At least two of them are still here – clearing up, I suppose. They can do a couple of things with us – leave us and run, or get rid of us somehow. Martin and the immigrants must have got away. The police will find us eventually, so these people have to leave here, whatever they do with us. Do they take us with them or hope to disappear before we're found? We can identify them.'

'Which makes them very dangerous.'

'Quite. We need to get out of here before they get a bad idea. Sit back to back, and see if we can undo the knots. I'll try yours first.'

'No, I've a better idea.' Imogen lay on the cement floor and blew a few stalks of filthy straw from her face. She wriggled and twisted while Cuff watched in the half-light, admiring her flexibility. It did not look difficult for her to get her hands over her hips, pull both legs up and push her feet between her arms.

'Now I can see what I'm doing.'

Using her teeth, Imogen pulled her knots apart. She flexed her hands, gave him a triumphant grin and said, 'Now you.'

'Thanks. Can you give me a leg up? I'll get over the partition and unlock the door from the outside.'

Cuff stepped in her cupped hands and reached for the top of the wall. Once up, he used the roof tie above him to steady himself. A noise came from the front of the barn, and the door opened with a creak. There was a glow outside and the sound of an engine running. Cuff pulled himself up onto the thick oak beam and lay still.

'Lie down, hands behind your back. Quick. Someone's coming,' he whispered.

The man, his dog and his gun reached the stall door. He unbolted it and went in. Imogen was lying in the straw in front of him. He gestured at her to get up, and searched for Cuff in the darkness. He shouted something at her.

Cuff dropped. He hit the man on his shoulders, knocking him flat. He grabbed the greasy ponytail and yanked it back then slammed his head onto the floor, and again.

The dog leapt. An excruciating pain shot through his forearm as the teeth sank in. He tucked his head in to protect his throat. The dog was worrying its prize, shaking its powerful head from side to side and growling furiously. His flesh was going to rip apart. His grip on the ponytail had weakened. But he had to keep hold of the man, who was fighting under Cuff's weight, the gun still in his right hand.

Imogen was on her feet beside him. She had trapped the dog's hind quarters between her legs and grabbed its collar from behind. Both her hands were trying to lift the animal and twist the collar to choke it. The dog was rasping, but its jaws were locked. Imogen's grunts in her effort to twist harder added to the noise.

At last the dog broke its hold, but she couldn't let go, or it would return to the attack. '*Stop*, you bugger. Stop fighting. Hurry, Cuff, hurry. I can't hold on much longer.'

The man was trying to get the gun round to point at his attacker. Cuff slammed his head into the floor again, kept doing it. His left arm wouldn't work, there was nothing beyond the pain. Adrenalin and desperation to keep the gun away, to smash this man into unconsciousness, drove out all other sensations.

He took a risk. He let go of the man's head and grabbed the gun with his right hand, ripped it free. He rammed the muzzle into the hair below the ponytail.

'Stop your dog, or I'll kill it.'

'*Go to hell.*' The words were a weak shout into dust on the floor.

Pointing it away from Imogen, Cuff put the gun to the dog's head. The weapon shook in his hands. 'No. I can't do this. Can you hold on for a minute more?'

Imogen grunted.

He took that as a yes. He struggled to pick up one of the lengths of rope with his left hand. It wouldn't work. Dog-man was still lying face down. Cuff slipped the shells out of the breach to prevent an accidental discharge, snapped the gun shut and reversed it. He slammed the butt down hard on the man's head.

He put the rounds back in the breach and closed the gun again. Gathering the rope off the floor, he threaded it through the dog's collar and managed single-handedly to tie the end to the stall structure, leaving no slack.

'Let go and jump back.'

She did. The dog whipped round, snarling. Teeth grazed her hand, drool landed on her arm, but the rope checked its leap. It was too exhausted to fight. It stood with its head low, rasping in its struggle for air. Cuff took the other piece of rope, and together they lashed the man's hands behind his back and to his feet. Digging through Dog-man's jacket, he found two more shotgun cartridges and put them in his own pocket.

'He came in here to kill us. That would take two shots. There's another man somewhere waiting for those bangs. Block your ears, then we're getting out of here.'

They crawled out of the hole in the wall, ears still ringing from the shots which Cuff had fired into the floor near the Dog-man's head out of sheer malice.

They ran for the road, looking back every now and then and listening for pursuit.

Martin reached home somewhere around midnight. He knocked on his own front door. Ginny looked terrible as she opened it, but her face lit up as she rushed down the steps and held him so tight he could hardly breathe. She pulled him inside and looked him over, at the chain. 'What the hell is that? You've blood on your face. What happened? Where've you been? Poof, you stink.'

'I have to contact Cuff, tell him I'm all right.'

'I'll do that, you get clean, for God's sake – no, for *my* sake. God isn't interested in idiots.'

He unwound the chain and stripped his clothes off while she ran the hot water. He showered as Ginny, her fears for him put to rest, told him exactly what she thought of Cuff and him and his stupid behaviour, and didn't he think of the danger he was putting himself in, and what effect that would have on her if he had been hurt or killed? He stayed under the shower for ten minutes and in all that time, Ginny only repeated herself once. She was still going at him when she threw a towel in his direction.

'I can't reach Cuff. I'm going to bed. You can try again in the morning.' She stalked off.

Martin grinned to himself. All would be forgiven once she had her anger under control. Naked, he laid the tail of the chain on the floor before moving in beside her. He put out a tentative hand. Suddenly she laughed. 'Is this what they call bondage?' she murmured as she rolled on top of him.

Cuff had not slept at all. They had walked all the way back to the airfield, where he had broken a window and got to the office telephone. An ambulance picked them up and took them to hospital where his arm was cleaned, stitched and dressed. He was given a tetanus shot and a box of antibiotics. He tried to get Imogen to go home to bed, but she insisted on staying and going with him to report to the police, which was as dawn broke. Cuff was too pumped up to sleep and went into work as normal, but late.

He was summoned. Connor indicated a chair. 'Please sit.'

This wasn't the first time Cuff had noticed a softening in Connor's attitude to people. He did not normally say 'please' to his staff, but over the past week he had been more affable. What had happened to crack that gruff exterior?

It took over half an hour for Cuff to tell him what had happened and to deny being responsible for the night flights.

'It wasn't me, but I was aware of it and I've been trying to find out who it is.'

'Why didn't you tell me?'

'Because I thought it might have been you.'

Near the end, before he finished, Connor's attention wandered. He was looking past his junior instructor and into the crew room, his jaw muscles working hard. Cuff followed his gaze. Sonia and Jimmy were standing close together and chatting. Both had smiles on their faces, a rare phenomenon for Sonia. It was a while before Connor said thank you and dismissed him.

Imogen arrived at the school not long afterwards. 'I couldn't sleep.'

She looked tired but energetic, and very pretty. Yesterday evening's working together as a team, with the instructor–student relationship put aside, had drawn them closer together.

His tone had a greater familiarity to it than before. 'How are you after all that excitement?'

Her smile in return was warm. 'I'm good, actually, fired up for the next fight – my fight.'

'Talking of which, let's have a meeting over a beer at The Gargoyle this evening to discuss this trafficking and your battle. Martin and Ginny will be there, as my plan involves them too.'

'Great. May I ask Melissa to come too?'

'Of course. But please emphasise to her that this matter is highly confidential at the moment. It's as sensitive to the flying school as your problem with your stalker is to you, so she must promise to keep quiet.'

'You've had an idea about the stalker?'

'I'll tell you this evening with the others.'

The Gargoyle was synonymous with the swans which kept stationary against the current, casting hungry looks at the patrons on the deck over the river. Cuff secured a table at the water's edge, and Martin went to the bar to order the drinks. They had all arrived at the same time and introductions had been made in the car park.

'Do these two girls know what's going on, Cuff?' There was a hard edge to Ginny's voice.

Ginny was easy to read in these circumstances. Cuff braced himself. 'Imogen does, I told her yesterday and she dived in the deep end. Melissa, no. She's about to find out everything, though, because I'm also involved in a sordid problem of theirs, for which I need your help.'

'We'll see about that. I need to add to what I said to you on Wednesday. Do you have any idea of the state Martin came home in last night? Do you have any idea what your bloody stupid plan could have done?'

She turned to Imogen. 'Martin comes home with a bloody chain locked round his waist, blood all over his face and that black eye. And it's this man who again – yes, again – is responsible and drags Martin, who is too bloody stupid and loyal to say no, into these scrapes. If you value your life, treat Cuff like the plague if he looks as if he's going to get involved in something dodgy. He gives me stomach ulcers.'

Cuff put on a suitably chastened expression and suppressed his smile. Ginny's words were both sincere and correct, but she would forgive him in a few moments.

He leaned across the table and kissed her on the cheek. 'Bloody man,' she growled, but then broke down and laughed, stretching out a hand to him. She grabbed his right arm and pointed to the livid scars. 'These, Imogen, are the direct result of his stupidity. They're on the left one as well, under that bandage.'

'I've been wanting to ask you about those. How on earth did you get them?'

'Lion,' said Cuff.

Ginny rolled her eyes. Melissa scoffed at him, and Imogen shook her head in negative acceptance.

'Would you believe me if I said … a bear?'

'No, not lion, or bear. Where did they come from?'

'I will tell you, but not now. I need to explain what's going on.'

Martin returned, followed by a waitress with a tray of drinks.

Cuff outlined the whole immigrant trafficking issue as he

saw it, adding, 'We told the police what happened last night. It took them a while, but they raided the farm this morning. The slavers had gone, unsurprisingly. Hopefully they'll catch them somewhere. They arrested three illegal immigrants in the woods, though.'

Martin shook his head. 'Only three? There were five there; two must have escaped. I wonder which ones they were.' He paused and added, 'I feel so bad about that. I promised I wouldn't report them, and they'll think it was me.'

There was silence. Cuff had his own opinion, but were the others debating internally what they would have done – been patriotic and reported the illegals, or been humanitarian and helped them, or both?

Imogen said, 'Do you have no clue who the pilot is?'

'No. Connor gave the police a group photo of all the instructors, so hopefully one of their prisoners will be able to identify him. To be honest I had a brief thought it was you at one stage, because you were coming in to fly looking tired and could have been up all night.'

Imogen laughed. 'Me? I don't have the skill or the courage to go night flying like that. No, I'm not sleeping well at the moment because this bastard has been ringing me at all hours and I'm worried where it's all going to end.' She turned to Martin and Ginny. 'I'm being stalked. I thought it was Cuff to start with, but I'm over that. We're thinking of ways to find out who he is.'

'Cuff?' Ginny and Martin both laughed. 'He's a bloody menace, but he's not perverted, I promise you.'

Cuff looked at them all in turn. 'The time has come to help Imogen, and I'm going to tell you what I think should be done to catch this stalker. He's been lurking on the roof above my flat and taking photographs when the full moon shines into Imogen's place across the road. We need to finalise a plan now, because the full moon will be up tomorrow. The weather forecast is not good, unfortunately, with cloud cover and a high chance of rain. If tomorrow is washed out, we'll carry it forward to next month unless some other avenue to catch him presents itself. Ginny and Martin, we'll need your help, please.'

Ginny thumped the table in confirmation. 'You see what I mean? He's going to involve all of us in some crazy scheme which will stretch the bounds of legality and cause death and destruction. And we're going to be stupid enough to go along with it and help. I need another drink.'

16

18–25 August

As predicted, the cloud cover on Saturday night had been absolute, low and accompanied by drizzle. Disappointed and hoping that postponing the plan to trap the stalker until the next full moon on the 15th of September would not affect its success, Cuff walked into the crew room and went straight to the coffee machine. He had got up very early and now needed a boost. His bitten arm was painful and stiff, but would not stop him flying.

He deliberated over what type of beverage he wanted, then pressed the buttons for an espresso. A small huddle of students were talking in hushed tones and casting looks in his direction. Did he look as if he had just got out off bed? One of them left the group and approached as the final drops plopped into his cup.

'Cuff.' Mr Keen seemed a little nervous. 'Er, we heard you had an accident once?'

'True, I did, but it was a long time ago. What of it?'

'Er, um, well … we thought you could tell us about it in case we could learn something. Everyone's very curious.'

'I could do, but there's not much to learn. I was just bloody lucky to get away with it.' Cuff collected his cup, and Mr Keen went away.

Later, Cuff interrupted as Craig was leaning over Imogen and trying to charm her. 'I've noticed for a couple of days now, some students are not meeting my eye and avoiding me, but I feel their stares following me.'

'Someone posted on Facebook that you had an accident a while back,' Imogen said. 'The comment claims you had an engine fire, panicked and made a botch of the whole emergency. It says the fire was manageable and you wrecked a perfectly good aircraft.'

Cuff stared at her in disbelief. 'Why on earth would someone say something like that and tell the world about it? What do you think? Don't tell me you believe it?'

'No, I don't. I have to admit it had me concerned for a short while, but I got over it, and after the other day I certainly don't believe you would panic to the extent of crashing.'

Thank God. Her support means a hell of a lot to me, more than I would have thought.

Craig agreed. 'Neither do I. I wouldn't take any notice of the students. For the record, I'd say some monkey is having a go at you. I'm on Facebook, so I'll comment on that post if you like.'

'Thanks, Craig, that's good of you. Look, I freely admit I panicked, but I challenge anyone to say they wouldn't have done in those circumstances. And the story of a plain engine fire is far too simplistic. I have the Aviation Authority accident report at home, I'll show it to you.'

'That'd be nice,' Imogen answered. 'You know what people are like. The other students want to believe the worst. I think you should tell them exactly what happened. Come out in the open and shoot down the liar.'

'Not a bad idea, but why should I have to defend myself in public? Who is this individual who claims to know all about it?'

'I don't know, it's some nom de plume.'

'More of this creepy stuff.' Imogen stretched out to hand the phone to her friend. 'This is from the original number, Jekyll's.'

Melissa frowned and read the text out loud. '"*Your nipples will harden at the gentle teasing of my fingers.*"'

'There's more, scroll down.'

'"*I feel the smooth, creamy skin of your inner thighs.*"'

'More.'

'"*I will lick off the sweat gracing the valley between your breasts after our sex. Soon my love, soon.*"' Melissa handed the phone back, her lips set in a thin line. 'This is disgusting. Actually, we could see it as harmless but annoying were it not for Mr Hyde's threatening messages from the other phone.'

'I'm getting more scared as these messages pile up. On the other hand I want to find him and fight him. This man is sick, and sick people do bad things. I've got to get him first.'

As promised, Cuff had arranged a session of aerobatics with Sonia in a special aircraft over at Casewell, where he had access to one, thanks to Martin's father. It had been a good flight and Sonia was in an ebullient mood, something Cuff had never before witnessed. He was pleased he had found something to coax warmth from that cool exterior. It wasn't that he was fond of her, it was about feeling good to have a positive effect on someone. On the drive back and after they had exhausted a detailed examination of their efforts, Cuff broached the first of two subjects he needed to talk through with someone more experienced. 'Sonia, apparently there's a post on Facebook which calls my judgement and temperament into question when I had my accident.'

'I've seen it, and so have all the students.'

'What are they saying?'

'I don't listen to gossip and I don't take much notice of what's on social media. Most of it is tripe. However, I did hear some students gossiping and agreeing they were glad you're not their instructor. I interrupted and told them we don't employ people who can't cope under pressure.'

'Thank you. What do you think, though? Do you believe the post?'

'I don't, and the post looks suspect to me, but I'm very cynical. You need to lay everyone's suspicions to rest. Brief them.'

'That's what Imogen said.'

'Then do it.'

'I'll do better than that. I'll post a copy of the accident report on the notice board. That's official, and I won't have to stand up and defend myself.'

Sonia nodded her approval. 'I did ask Connor what he thought, and he told me your instructor at the time had given him the full story, so don't worry on that score.'

'Thank you. Another thing,' Cuff said. 'You know these night flights which have been taking place?'

She shrank into her dour shell. 'What of it?'

'I'm sure Connor's told you someone accused me of taking the Cessna. I'm not worried, because I can prove I didn't. I don't know how much you know, Sonia, but I found out about it by accident, and in trying to learn who the pilot was I discovered this business of immigrant trafficking and slavery.

I thought it was Connor at first, because I saw his car at the office when I was lurking round the airfield at midnight.'

Sonia snorted a brief laugh. 'Not Connor – it was probably me. I had a couple of physio appointments and came in to work late on those days. Connor was away so I borrowed his car, but I ran home and ran back the next day to pick it up. I have an idea who is stealing the aircraft, though.'

'Really, who?'

'I was working late on something early last month. I run to and from work. I don't have a car, so no one knows whether I'm there or not. On that night, everyone had gone home, or so I thought. There was a noise in the reception. I crept to the door and looked around and saw someone taking one of the aircraft keys. I couldn't see which one. He did something close to his chest with his back to me, then put the keys back and closed the cupboard. He went out and locked the door behind him, so it was someone from the school.'

'Who?'

'I can't say for sure, he was wearing a hoodie, so I never saw his face.' Sonia paused, then added, 'It could have been a woman, I suppose.'

Something in her voice as well as that final sentence, which might have been added to create doubt, made Cuff think she was lying.

He took his eyes from the road for a moment and shot her quick glance. 'Who was it, Sonia?'

She was studying him, anxiety written across her face. That was not surprising: her concern would always be the welfare and reputation of the school itself, so she'd be desperate to keep it quiet. Craig, Jimmy, Mike, even Connor – the exposure of any one of them would be harmful publicity.

Cuff, Craig and Jimmy were standing at the door of a briefing room when Mike Penny came out of Connor's office, his usual buoyant and cocky self. He was limping slightly, but was not wearing his support boot.

The impressionable students amongst the usual morning gathering crowded round him. 'How did the flight test go, Mike?'

'Did you have a test?'

'Everyone's got to have a test before flying if they've been off for medical reasons or been away too long. Yeah, it went well; aced it, in fact.'

Cuff shook his head. 'How does he have the gall to blow his own trumpet the way he does?'

Jimmy sneered. 'No one else is going to tell everyone how wonderful he is, so he's got to do it himself – prick.'

Mike came over to the other instructors and pushed between them to talk to Cuff. 'I'm back ...'

'I see that.'

'So I'll take Imogen back and bring her up to skills test standard. I'll 'ave to undo some of the stuff yer've taught her.'

God, you're a pathetic little squirt. Aloud, Cuff said, 'Which instructor she has is her and Connor's decision, not yours. If she wants to come back to you, which I doubt, it's no skin off my nose. Actually, she's doing rather well, and she'll be taking her test on Monday. She has the hours now. Apparently you teach your students to be 'positive' on the controls. When I first took her on, she was rough with the machine, over-controlling, with the result she had to make more corrections than necessary. She's now very smooth, and it's a pleasure to fly with her.'

'Yer've got a bloody cheek to criticise me. Yer still in fucking nappies. Connor made a serious mistake with yah. Yah don't know what yer fucking talking about. Yer've never taken a student this far. She wasn't anywhere near ready when I dropped out. She can't have improved that quickly. She needs more fucking time with me to get her right.'

'As I said, that's Connor's and Imogen's decision. In any case Sonia has agreed to assess her over the weekend to see whether it's worth her taking her skills test. You should leave it up to a more experienced person to judge.'

Mike looked as if he was about to hit the bigger man, but turned to see Imogen standing in the doorway, Craig behind her. She was plainly cross. He grabbed her arm to lead her back into the room. She shook his hand off, but followed. Cuff moved around the pair and joined Craig outside.

Mike pushed at the briefing room door to shut out the other two, but it failed to close. Cuff was unashamedly interested in what Mike had to say and kept within earshot.

Imogen and Mike were about the same height. His head was thrust forward, hers was upright and defiant. His voice was raised, hers was soft and even.

'What's going on? Yer not gonna fly again with that bloke are yah? He ain't got enough experience to put yah up for yer test. I've told yah, yah need a few more hours to sharpen up.'

'Cuff says I'm ready and I believe him. In any case, it'll be up to Sonia to judge, so why don't you wait and see. I've been getting on well with him, and I feel a lot more confident. I'm not switching instructors again at this late stage.'

'Yah don't know what yer talking about, and neither does he.' He stabbed a finger in Cuff's direction.

'Mike, your trouble is you're always trying to control me. It took me a long time to realise that, but it's not going to work any more. I won't have you telling me what to do. So even if Sonia says I'm not ready, my flying will continue with Cuff, because he's teaching me well and not trying to dominate me.'

'Yah haven't got a fucking clue!'

Cuff edged closer to the open door. Imogen's control was admirable. She was keeping the temperature of this argument down, while Mike was heating it up. But he must have triggered something, because she suddenly went on the attack.

She took a step forward, and he was forced to retreat. She was almost nose to nose with him. 'And one other thing. I want absolutely nothing more to do with you. You will stop sending me texts. You will stop telling me what 'we' are going to do. You will stop trying to win me back and stop your pathetic suggestions about sex. Go away and let me live my life in the way I choose. No more; nothing – is that clear?'

Mike was quivering. His mouth moved but no words came out; his arms were still at his sides, but his fists clenched and opened repeatedly. Abruptly he turned and stormed out of the room, pushing his way between Cuff and Craig. His final words were loud. 'Yer making a big mistake.'

Pad, pad, pad, pad, pad. Sonia was not going to run too far, she didn't have time today, so she forced a faster pace than normal.

She was feeling satisfied and smiled to herself. Her life was turning around. From being the grumpy spinster with no future, she was unexpectedly emerging as a cheerful woman who was approaching middle age with a positive and optimistic attitude. This was due to two factors which had coincided within a short space of time.

She was now a partner in the school with an increased salary, and since seizing that power from Connor her personal life had taken a turn for the better as well.

Jimmy had asked for training advice as he wanted to start running. Since then they had chatted more and grown closer. Nothing had developed so far – Jimmy was a bit scared of women in spite of the way he fooled about – but they gravitated towards each other when at the school, shared coffee and ate their meagre lunches together. Jimmy made her laugh so much more than she had ever done. He made her feel appreciated as a woman. Others, except Mike, were pleasant, but Jimmy's attention was more fulfilling. In fact, even if nothing further developed with him, Jimmy had already replaced Connor in her life.

These two elements gave her the strength to assert herself and to control Connor as she deserved. For once she had the whole world at her mercy.

And, to top it all, she was in a position to receive a tidy lump sum.

It was interesting, the way that man had responded when she accused him of hiding flights in the Cessna. His initial reaction was anger: she was a liar and was making it all up because she thought him contemptible. But she had kept calm and presented her evidence to him in a logical and irrefutable way. When he saw she was deadly serious and knew almost everything, his argument collapsed. What she freely admitted that she didn't know was where exactly he had collected the illegals. France, of course, but where? That, he didn't say.

Nevertheless, he went to pieces. He was beaten and guilty and scared silly about what was going to happen to him. He had never done anything immoral or dishonest in his life before, he insisted. He was driven to doing it because he desperately needed the money; a sentiment she could easily share.

He was so nervous over whether she was going to report him, that without thinking of the consequences of revealing it, he even told her how much he was being paid for smuggling migrants.

From that moment it was easy. He wasn't facing a rap over the knuckles for this crime, she had pointed out, he was facing a lengthy jail term. But she would keep his secret for a cut of his payment; not an excessive amount, she emphasised, just thirty per cent. He told her he had the money and would pay her straightaway. She gave him a deadline. It had been so satisfying to witness the deflation of his balloon of arrogance.

A small doubt niggled at her, though, and it was a worry. She had a strong suspicion that at least one of the two nefarious activities she had discovered was going to continue, perhaps both. If she denounced either of them she would be breaking her word, and the results would be catastrophic for the school, and the school was everything. Exposure would be ugly – there would be time in court and unwanted publicity. Hence the blackmail: a small sum to show him she meant what she said. He must stop or be reported. That way, she imagined the whole episode would die a natural death and the school would not suffer.

On the other hand, her dilemma was she had a legal duty to report the crimes, and, as they were both immoral and criminal, she really ought to go to the police.

17

25–30 August

Imogen left the briefing room where Cuff had been trying to settle her nerves by telling her she had nothing to worry about with her skills test as long as she flew normally. Mike approached, evidently in a cheerful mood. His temper tantrum of five days ago long over, he appeared to have put the episode behind him.

As Imogen came abreast of him he put out a hand to stop her. She pushed it away, but faced him. Without a hint of remorse for his previous behaviour, he said, 'Imo, I just want to say good luck for yer test. How yah feeling?'

She was used to his utter lack of embarrassment over anything, as he switched moods to suit his preferred outcome as easily as changing his socks. Nevertheless, the last outburst had been particularly strong and she marvelled at how he appeared so concerned. 'Thanks, Mike, that's sweet of you. I feel good about it, actually, but I admit I'm a little nervous. But you said I wasn't ready – why the change of tune?'

'Ah, maybe I was a bit harsh. Maybe I demand too high a standard. Yah flew with Sonia and she's confident, so there yah go.' Mike held out a small tin. 'Here, have a biscuit for strength. Take two. Don't worry, it'll go well. No probs.'

'Thanks, I skipped breakfast, so I'm pretty hungry now.'

'Have three – take a bunch.'

'Two's plenty.' Imogen smiled at him. He could be quite gracious if he tried.

'Five minutes, Imogen,' Connor called from his office.

She was about to meet her maker. 'Ooh, here we go. I must go to the loo before the flight. I'll see you later, Mike.'

'Great. When yer've passed I'll take yah up for aerobatics. I'm into that now, yer'll love it.'

Probably not, and I don't need that thought to add to my worries. I have to calm my nerves, they're destroying me. It's ridiculous and solely due to self-imposed pressure. Following a career in which my skill is tested every six months will be impossible if I'm going to react like this every time. It'll be a nightmare.

Once she was in the machine and focused on the flight she would be all right, but she found the chief instructor's silent presence unnerving. While she carried out the preflight inspection, calling out what she was looking at, he made notes on his clip-board. What had she done wrong, what vital factor had she missed? Why was he making comments already?

Once airborne after a normal take-off, she settled down and concentrated on flying smoothly and accurately. She could pass this test easily if it wasn't for her nerves.

The navigation part of the test went by without a problem. By the time it was over, she had regained confidence and ceased to worry.

Connor told her to do a series of basic flight manoeuvres which she reckoned were faultless. The last one, a steeply banked turn through a full 360 degrees, ended a bit wobbly. Her slightly excessive control inputs were puzzling. She didn't do that anymore, not since Cuff had induced her to fly smoothly.

She knew it was going to come at some stage, maybe more than once, but as she glanced out to her left before a turn, Connor pulled the throttle back, simulating engine failure. Imogen had dealt with this dozens of times. Not only that, but she had successfully coped with that real dead-stick landing with Cuff. Now, she went through the procedure and lowered the nose to maintain speed – she did it harshly and pushed too far. A moment later, she corrected and established the glide. She sought a field to make a forced landing, found one and manoeuvred to a position from where she could make an approach.

Why was the field moving? It would not stay still. Was it the field or was she rolling the aeroplane? Something wasn't right. Why couldn't she set this up properly? She was over-controlling, going too fast and then too slow. This rough handling was losing precious height. She wasn't going to make the pasture if she carried on like this.

There was a line of poplars across the approach at the edge of the field. The Cessna was never going to clear them. But she did nothing about it. Her stare was fixed on the trees as their image crept up the windshield. She was getting too low. What to do? The whole situation was confusing.

Connor was calm. He stowed his clip-board in the door pocket. 'I have control.' He opened the throttle and turned away from the trees. When they were clear he said, 'We're going back.'

Imogen slumped in her seat. She turned her head to stare out of the left window, seeing nothing and stemming tears which threatened. She took no notice of Connor flying. A blanket of failure smothered every part of her.

Back in the parking area, she stumbled out of the machine and grabbed the door for support before trailing behind Connor as they returned to the school building. Her footfall seemed exaggerated, thumping onto the tarmac, sending shock waves through her body. What had gone wrong? How could she have been handling the aircraft so badly?

Connor had said nothing up to that point, maintaining his customary aloofness. Once in his office, though, he told her to sit. 'How do you take your coffee?'

'Um, er … er, white, no sugar, please.' *Why did I have to think about that?*

Mike's grinning face and questioning look greeted her through the door window. She ignored him and looked for Cuff; he should be there for the debrief. No, he was going out, not expecting them to return until at least two hours had elapsed.

'Are you feeling all right, Imogen? You began the session very well, and I thought it was going to be an exceptional flight, but you panicked when I failed the engine, and you completely misjudged the approach. To make matters worse, you committed the unforgivable sin of landing downwind. Were you aware of the wind direction?'

Imogen sniffed and managed to stifle her desire to cry. 'I don't know, I just don't know. I was feeling fine, but then the aircraft went ahead of me. It was doing things, and I failed to correct it. I was too slow, I felt confused and didn't even consider the wind. I've never done that before. I'm so sorry.'

'I had to take control to stop us from hitting those trees. I'm afraid that automatically means you have failed. You do understand, don't you?'

'Yes, and you're right. I'll have to try again. I don't know what happened. All I know is it was fuzzy, I couldn't appreciate what was wrong, I was confused. I still am.'

'It was out of character, Imogen. If you've ever had spells like this at any other time, you should go and see a specialist.'

'No, and it hasn't gone away. I see what's going on, but my brain is taking time to catch up.'

Melissa poured two glasses of wine. It was early, but after the skills test disaster this was an exceptional circumstance. 'How do you feel now?'

Imogen was lying on her couch. Abruptly she jumped up and paced the room. 'Water, I need water, I'm so thirsty.' She filled a glass, put it down and paced the room once more. 'Didn't I pour water? I'm so thirsty.'

'Imo, you haven't drunk it. It's on the counter, and it's less than a minute since you poured it. Your eyes are red, girl. What have you been doing?'

'Oh God! Cuff is going to be so cross with me. He's going to do something terrible to me, and I deserve it. What do I do? I don't want to see him, I'm going to hide.'

'*Imo!* Pull yourself together. This is not like you at all. You're getting anxious over something which is never going to happen. Cuff won't do anything to you. Actually, he will most likely be supportive.' She patted the couch. 'Lie down.'

Imogen did as she was told, and Melissa took her pulse. 'This is racing. What's wrong with you, my girl? I might just call an ambulance.'

'No, I don't need that. I'm okay, I think. A bit fuzzy … slow thinking. How come I can realise that but be unable to do anything about it? My eye drops are in the bathroom, please get them. What's the time?'

'Just after five.'

'It can't be. I've been home for hours.'

'Fifteen minutes actually. Look, you didn't fail your test due to your inability, you failed because something was the matter with you, so there's no need to feel bad. Be disappointed, but don't lose faith in yourself. Cuff says you're good, he told me so, and you said Sonia complimented you on your flight with her. You'll take the test again and sail through.' Melissa went to answer a knock on the door, and let Cuff in.

He went over to Imogen and stood over her. She returned his look and burst into tears. 'I'm so sorry, Cuff. Your first student to be put up for a skills test, and I fail. I've not only let myself down, but you as well. Mike said I wasn't ready, and he was right. I've shown you up. I'm thirsty.'

Cuff shook his head. 'No. Absolutely not. What happened? Something did, you were not going to fail that test.' He nodded his thanks to Melissa as she gave him a glass of wine and Imogen her water.

Imogen repeated her story for Cuff's benefit, dragging it out, as if struggling to remember detail. 'You know what struck me as strange was Connor. I was expecting him to put me down, because he's like that. But he was kind, sort of fatherly. It was most unlike what we all think of him.'

Melissa was sitting in the only other chair. Imogen moved her legs to make space so Cuff could perch on the edge of the couch.

'What did you do today that was different from any other day?'

Imogen stared at him blankly for a moment. 'Nothing.'

Cuff stood. 'I have to go, I just came by to see how you are. Don't get too depressed. I promise you whatever happened wasn't anything to do with your ability. Remember how well you reacted to a real engine failure? And the rest of that night in the woods? You were able and confident and kept your head throughout. Those attributes were never going to allow you to fail. No, some other influence was at work. The next time will prove me right. Thanks for the wine, girls.'

Melissa closed the door behind Cuff and regarded her friend, shrugged and poured herself another glass of wine. Imogen returned her look through barely open lids, before drifting off to sleep.

She woke an hour later with a stiff neck. Melissa was fuzzily happy by then, but she established that her patient was feeling better and stood behind her. 'Here, I'll give you a massage.'

'Ow! That hurts.'

'Ha-ha! All good massages hurt. Cuff is one super guy, you know, and he cares about you.'

'Ow! He is nice, but he's only interested in me as a student. He wants me to succeed because if I fail it reflects on him.'

'Rubbish, Imo. Don't be so cynical. You need to stop keeping him at arm's length and let him accept you as the gorgeous creature you are.'

Imogen laughed. 'Stop it. No, not the massage. Stop trying to butter me up, and stop trying to find me a boyfriend. I'm taking a break after Mike. Between him and the stalker, I'm totally off men for a while. If you think Cuff's so super, go for him yourself.'

'I bloody well would if I thought he'd be interested, but he's focused on you. You can see it in his face and his manner. He's protective of you. He's genuinely concerned over this stalker as well as your future as a pilot.'

'I'll see how I feel if he approaches me. But I don't think he's going to do that until I've passed, anyway. He would consider it unprofessional.' Imogen paused for a moment. 'Actually, when we were being chased in the woods and hiding under a tree trunk, our heads were touching.' She patted the top of her head to illustrate what she meant. 'I wanted to move at one point. The men were getting close, so he put his hand on my head and stopped me. He left his hand there, I remember the warmth of it. If you'd asked me, I would have said he should have moved it after the first contact, but I was quite comfortable with it being left there. Strange.'

'Not strange at all, Imo. Follow your instincts.'

'Cuff! I thought I'd find you here.'

'Hello, Melissa, what brings you into a pub on your own?' His eyes teased her. 'On the hunt?'

She was wearing a dark-green top, which showed off her copious waves of hair. They bounced on her shoulders as she laughed. 'No, I was looking for you, actually.'

'Oh, so I'm your prey, am I?'

'Be careful, Cuff, I might just pounce on you one day. How's your arm?'

'It's good, thanks. Dressing's off, and I've got full function. It's a bit sore if I strain with it, though. Drink?' He waved at the barmaid.

'House wine, thanks; white. Now, jokes aside. I love my friend, she's absolutely the best thing in my life, and I'll do anything for her. She doesn't show it much, but she's been pretty stressed by the stalker, the threats, and Mike's annoying attempts to get her back, and all this had been going on long before the test failure. That has had a huge impact on her morale. She's careless around the flat, throwing things about or dropping them. She's become untidy, which is unlike her, and she's nervous when we go out, looking over her shoulder. We've got to get to the bottom of this stalker thing, and quickly.'

'I didn't realise; she puts a good front on things. When we were in the woods she had her wits about her. It was good. The trouble is neither the police nor we have any way of identifying the creep until he leaves us a clue. If the idea I outlined to you all doesn't work, we'll have to wait for him to slip up. Until then we can give her support and never leave her alone.'

'I know. You could be more help, though.'

'What? How?'

'When are you going to wake up and see she thinks you're the best thing in the male kingdom?'

'Oh rubbish, Melissa. I don't deny we get on well, but she's totally focused on her career and not interested in men. Our relationship is one with a bit of distance between us – friendly, but not too close. She's not made one single comment or gesture to me which was not professional. Besides which, I'm not very trusting of relationships myself, not after my brief and disastrous marriage. It's left me very wary.'

'Oh … Of course. I'm interfering in your lives … but it's only because I can see how good you two are for each other. I promise you, Cuff, there's not a horrid bone in Imogen at all. She would truly benefit from closer contact with you. Please believe me.'

He nodded and smiled at her. 'Cheers. You mean well, so thanks for that. Time will sort everything out.'

18

30 August – 01 September

Cuff had a couple of consecutive vacant slots in his programme and had agreed to meet Martin for a coffee. He was early and seated at a table by the door.

Martin passed the window and waved. He went straight to the counter to order – he didn't need to ask Cuff what he wanted after all the time they'd known each other.

Martin put the tray on the table. 'How's it going?'

'There's something odd going on in my life – I think. A few things have happened recently which are making me uncomfortable, suspicious even, but I'm not sure if there's anything wrong or not.'

'What do you mean?'

'I have the feeling someone is trying to discredit me. Someone told Connor I was stealing the aircraft and smuggling migrants; someone posts on Facebook about my supposed failings with my crash; and the other day Connor called me in to tell me there have been complaints that I've left the aircraft in a mess and made errors in the log book – all of which is blatantly untrue. And then Imogen uncharacteristically failed her skills test for a reason we can't understand. I'm thinking her failure was engineered somehow and she wasn't the only target – the other was me.'

'You have an incredible ability to get yourself into crazy situations, don't you. Look at this trafficking thing. You didn't have to get involved, you could have gone straight to the police instead of trying to do something about it yourself.'

'Martin, you're being a prick. I had every intention of going to the police, but you went and got yourself deep in the poo. It was you who dragged me in.'

Martin laughed. 'Yes, sorry. It had you being a "Jonathan" though, didn't it?'

'Instinct, that's all. Anyway, I've so far managed to convince Connor I'm not a smuggler, and I seem to have overcome the students' contempt for my panic by making the accident report available to them all. In fact a couple have told me they thought I did a great job in an uncontrollable situation, and others have shown respect instead of avoiding my eyes. So that's all good. But I'm worried about Imogen. There's her stalker, and she should never have failed that test. Something was wrong.'

Martin gave him a devilish grin. 'You're quite struck by her, aren't you. It matters to you what she thinks. Does she believe you?'

Cuff paused, thinking for a minute. 'She's great, but there's so much going on at the moment I've no time or inclination to pursue her.'

'You're such a liar. I can read you like a book. And it's time you got off your backside and did something about a woman.

I'm going to set Ginny on you; she'll get you mated.'

'Get back in your box, Martin. But you're right, it does matter to me what she thinks, because she's a nice person, and I don't want her to think I'm not fully competent. I'm sure she was suspicious after the Facebook post, although she didn't want to believe it. She's fully on side now, though.'

'So who's doing this, if it is actually a campaign?'

'The only one who springs to mind is Mike Penny. I have no proof, but he's a vindictive little sod who hates me and has been trying to keep control of Imogen.'

'What are you going to do now?'

'I'm going to the police. We've got to try to identify the pilot somehow.'

At the police station, Cuff asked for Detective Inspector Baker, the man he'd met with Ginny.

'Connor Royle gave you a group photo of all the instructors and staff at the school. Have your illegals identified the pilot?'

Baker pulled the photo from a file and slapped it on the desk. He stabbed a thick, blunt finger on the faces. 'Not conclusive, I'm afraid. One of them said it was this man and the other pointed to this one. The other pointed to you at first, then said he didn't recognise any of them.'

'It's definitely not him.' Cuff indicated Craig. 'I told you I only saw the man's figure, not his face, but Craig here is about six foot three, and the one I saw is much shorter than that. It could be any of the other men: Connor, Mike or Jimmy. I wondered if it could be a woman; the only three at the school are all about the right height, but slightly built. I don't see any of them being able to lift and hold a full jerry can of fuel, almost forty pounds, above their shoulders.'

'Thank you, Mister Scott, at least you've narrowed the field a little.'

* * *

'I forgot in all the excitement,' Martin said later. 'I asked them where they were going, where they'd been told was a safe place. Bardhyl, the one who undid the padlock, gave me this scrap of paper. It looks like a postcode.'

'I suppose they knew the name of the place and all they had to do was find it from this. Let's go and see what's there.'

Where a particular postcode starts and ends is a secret known only to postmen. Cuff was driving along the road as slowly as the traffic would allow. He used it sometimes on his way home from shopping although had taken little notice of the houses and businesses that lined it.

'What does a refuge for illegal immigrants look like?' Martin stared out of his window and reeled off the buildings. 'Dry cleaner, fish and chip shop ...'

Cuff was looking out his side. 'Polish delicatessen, second-hand furniture shop.'

'Flats? There's no way of telling what's hidden behind the store fronts.'

'We're coming up to the traffic light. All that's left is the White Hart pub and a hand car wash. The car wash! I know this place.' Cuff swung out of the road and into the forecourt. One vehicle was being washed, another waited.

Cuff pulled over to the side. 'Look at these workers. They all have a Mediterranean look to them. Where are they from? Let's go and talk to the boss.'

A heavy, bull-necked man came out of the caravan. He put on a salesman's broad forced grin and spread his arms in welcome. 'Yes, my friends. What wash you want today? This best hand car wash in UK. I make you a good deal. You sign week wash contract. Is very cheap and car always clean. More good is month contract – better value. How about it?'

Martin was watching the workers and looking around as Cuff engaged the boss. 'I'm sorry, I don't come this way often enough to sign a contract, but I know someone who does. Can you give me a list of prices?'

'Of course. Come to office.'

Cuff followed him and was about to step up into the doorway, when Martin yelled, '*Bardhyl.*'

A man was running with Martin after him. The boss lost his friendly face. The caravan door slammed shut. He screamed something in a foreign language. The workers stopped their wiping and stood looking down the street. A yellow bucket was on its side, foam spreading out over the tarmac. Cuff sprinted.

Martin tired. He was doubled over, one hand on a lamp post and gasping for air. Cuff reached him. It was pointless chasing any more because the runner had vanished, and Cuff didn't even know what he looked like.

'That was Bardhyl,' Martin panted, 'from the farm. Bloody hell. I never could run fast, now I've lost him.'

'It doesn't matter. This points a finger at Mike Penny. I saw him here talking to the boss, just before the night flights began. One of your Albanians has run away from here, and car washes are well known for using forced labour.'

'Hey, my friend. What going on? No trouble here. You want car wash or no?'

'Do you know the man that ran away?'

'I no see man.' He pointed and shouted something. Four labourers stood up around the car and were looking in their direction. 'All my men are here.'

'Let's go, Martin.'

The receptionist was regarding Imogen with sympathy – or was it pity? Mike was hovering behind her as she pored over the booking sheet, waiting for her to leave the counter, which was strange for him. He would normally have interrupted any conversation. He was fidgety and hesitant in his movements and had a rather glum air which he struggled to hide. He seemed depressed but covered it with exaggerated expressions in his face and speech.

'Imo baby, bad luck with your skills test. I was gobsmacked to hear. I warned yah, though, didn't I? Anyways, I thought I'd take yah on a trip. Make yah feel better.'

Imogen's neck muscles tensed again. She shook her head.

'Don't be negative. I forgive yah. Trip'll be great for yah. I'm gonna show yah a real special place. Its full beauty can only be seen from the air. It'll be an experience yer'll remember yer whole life.'

'No, Mike. I don't want to fly with you, and I certainly don't want you to demonstrate your aerobatic skills, if that's what this is all about. Why can't you ever take no for an answer? Why?'

'It's for your own good, Imo. Yah need to get a greater appreciation of life. Yer'll be thrilled to death, I promise yah. It's not aerobatics.'

'Mike, I said NO, and I mean NO. Now stop pestering me.'

'Okay, baby, yah don't leave me a choice. See these?' He handed her his camera. 'Scroll through.'

Imogen gasped. Heat flushed up into her cheeks. Three images were enough. She punched the camera back at his chest and let it drop.

He caught it, his lips twisting without humour. 'There's more, baby.' He wagged his finger at her. 'Either yah come with me, or ... well, yah can guess where these'll end up. Think hard. D'yah reckon yah could handle the exposure?'

'You creep! You sick bloody bastard!' Imogen's mouth curled in disgust.

'Yer one hundred per cent correct in that – my mum told me. Are yah coming, or not? A flying trip of a lifetime, or a lifetime of shame?'

'Where are you going to take me?'

'Think of this as one of those 'close yer eyes and hold out yer 'ands' kind of presents.' He turned away, took a square of paper from his pocket and pinned it to the notice board before leading her outside.

Cuff and Jimmy were drinking coffee and arguing over who was going to win the Six Nations rugby tournament in the upcoming season. They were idly watching Craig who, as safety officer, had the task of making sure all the information on the notice board was up to date, which meant old, well-read material was taken down and replaced with new and interesting stuff.

Jimmy stopped talking about Wales's prospects and pointed past Cuff's shoulder to the parking area. 'Looks like Imogen's going to fly with Mike. I thought that was all over.'

Cuff turned to see. 'So did I. I wonder what the hell's going on – she hasn't had a good word to say about him recently.'

Craig stopped glancing at old notices and took a sheet of paper off the board. It had been folded into four and could not be read without flattening it. He stepped back and opened it. 'I don't like this. There's a bad vibe in this letter.' He thrust it out for the other two to look at. It was done in a hurry, typed as if the writer couldn't be bothered to punctuate or capitalise most of it.

it wont be long before im found out. soon the police will come and everyone will know what ive done. ive done things that an instructor at this school shouldnt do but i did them bloody well. i had to do it to prove myself to myself. i tried hard to be better than everyone else and to get you all to respect me but instead you all looked down on me. i dont know

why but this is never going to change
ever. ill always have this fight. no one
will give me the respect i deserve. im
good, im bloody good but no one
recognises this. Why not?

im going to end it now before i have to
face the shame and before im punished. im
taking imo with me because shes my life.
she lives in my sight and in my dreams. i
cant live without her so she must come
to.

sorry i failed everyone. mike

sorry connor for your aircraft. I chose
the cheapest one

Cuff stared up at Craig and across to Jimmy. They stared back. No one moved, each trying to imagine the note was not what it appeared to be.

It was Cuff who snapped out of the daze first. 'That's a suicide letter!'

Two slow nods answered him, before the pair sprang into life.

'We've got to stop them.' Cuff glanced out of the window. Imogen and Mike had disappeared amongst the parked aircraft. 'Jimmy, tell Connor or Sonia. Craig, get on the radio. Tell Mike he's not permitted to take off. I'm going after them.'

'How?' Jimmy called to a closing door.

The little two-seat Cessna 150 was taxiing out of the parking area. It was moving at a normal speed towards the runway end. Cuff would never catch it by running. There had to be something he could use. The fire truck, a pickup with a big foam extinguisher and other equipment on the back, which was manned by volunteers at busy times, was too far away and in the wrong direction.

The Cessna was halfway to the runway. The school bicycle leaned against the wall. It was not a racing bike, nor the regular type everyone rode these days, but an old utility bike with rattling loose mudguards, a chain guard, rod-actuated brakes which squeaked, a bell which was stuck and a wicker basket which the engineers used to carry tools and small spares to the aeroplanes. Cuff grabbed it and stood on the pedals. He took a shortcut across the grass to reach the taxiway. Acceleration was slow. Everything about the bike was stiff, except for the rattling bits. *Christ, if the bloody engineers can look after the aircraft so well, why can't they oil the bloody bike?* Cuff never touched the saddle – instead he stood and stamped down on the pedals, swinging the machine from side to side in his desperation to speed up.

On the taxiway the surface was harder and he was gaining on the Cessna, but he was tiring. A hundred yards stood between it and the threshold; for Cuff, an additional fifty. *Imogen's in that aircraft!* He pushed himself harder and harder on the pedals until he could not do better. *Come on!*

Mike had reached the runway end. He slowed to take the turn and line the trainer up for take-off. Behind him, Cuff was only a few yards away. He dropped the bike without stopping, stumbled, jumped up and sprinted.

The engine note rose to a roar. The Cessna charged forward. The propeller wash buffeted Cuff as he leapt and landed over the horizontal surface of the tailplane. The leading edge was rounded and smooth under his locked fingers. The propeller's wind was fierce in his face, a whiff of exhaust fumes caught his nostrils. The toes of his shoes were bouncing on the ground. He raised his legs and humped himself up and further forward, leaving the lower part of his body over the elevators, holding them down.

19

01 September

When a hundred and eighty pound man crashes onto the tail of a tiny aircraft with a massive thump, it's going to be felt. The whole machine shook and shuddered. The nose went up, obscuring Imogen's view of the runway ahead. Mike pushed at the control column to correct, but it had been forced out of his hand to fully forward anyway. The nose stayed high.

Imogen turned to see through the rear window.

'It's Cuff, he's on the tail! Stop, he'll fall off. You'll kill him.'

Mike took a quick glance back and grinned. 'Fucking great. That's exactly what the useless bastard deserves. He can join us on our little trip, if he can hold on to the end. The very end!' His hysterical laughter surpassed the engine's roar, and Imogen suddenly understood.

'*Stop*. Please stop, Mike.'

Across the cockpit from Imogen, Mike's chin jutted forward. He was straining to see the runway round the side of the high nose. He was going to get airborne and nothing was going to stop him.

The Cessna was accelerating, but much slower than normal. It was heavily overweight, and was eating up runway fast. The nose was so high, the tail was scraping on the ground, creating a horrible noise that rumbled through the airframe. As it gained speed, the increasing wind over the elevators began to take effect, and the down pressure on the tail eased. But the nose stayed high. Mike was so obsessed with taking off, he didn't seem to understand what the effect of a man on the tail was having. With so much weight so far back, the aircraft would stall as soon as it left the ground; it would never fly.

This was madness. Imogen couldn't sit there and let things happen. She had to fight. The only thing she could do was shut the engine down, but Mike's right hand was covering the throttle. She reached for the fuel shut-off valve, but he smashed a backhand across her face, knocking her back. He did it again, harder. Every time he took his hand off the throttle to hit her, she tried to reach the fuel switch, but he got there first and held it firm. She grabbed his sleeve to pull his hand away. He let her, and followed the movement through to plant another backhander into her face.

She was livid. She was reeling, reaching forward and making grabs for the throttle or the fuel, but every time her hand came out he punched her, over and over again.

They reached flying speed. The remaining runway was diminishing.

He screamed his frustration. 'When I've got rid of this piece of fucking shit behind, I'm climbing to five thousand feet. Then, Imo, I'm gonna dive straight down, vertical, until we hit the ground at terminal velocity. You're gonna be screaming your lovely head off, and I'm going to be laughing mine off. We're gonna hit the ground headless. How's that?'

'Give up Mike, we're never going to take off. It'll never fly. It'll stall.'

'Fucking bastard!' he yelled. 'I'm not giving up. I'll shake him off.'

He kicked at alternate pedals to yaw the machine from side to side. Right went forward, left was stuck. Right – left jammed. Right – left … *'Bloody hell.'*

Cuff's body was not only holding the elevators down, it was up against the rudder, which would now only move in one direction. Imogen rammed her feet down onto the pedals and locked her legs straight. Mike planted yet another fist in her face.

Blood was streaming from her nose and her lip was split. Her life was at stake; Cuff's life was at stake. Furious, her pain became irrelevant.

'I've had enough of your crap.'

She twisted round and let fly with a flurry of blows to his head with both fists. He swore, but wasn't going to be put off. She hit him again and again, not letting up. They weren't effective blows, and at that stage he probably wasn't feeling pain, but they were too distracting to be ignored.

The runway end was approaching rapidly, and they were well over flying speed. There wasn't much distance left for the aeroplane to either stop or take off. Any moment and a tyre would burst or they would hit the boundary fence and crash through into the bushes beyond.

Cuff clung on. The wind was tearing at him, trying to drag him off. His fingers were locked onto the leading edge of the tailplane, but his dog-bitten left arm was feeling the strain. He had to hold his lower legs up: if he straightened them, his feet scraped the tarmac.

Mike's attempts to move the elevators pushed up at his lower body, but his weight held them down. The wind from the rising speed whipped about his face. Take-off was impossible, so only two things could happen: Mike would give up and cut the engine, or they would go faster and faster until they crashed, never having left the ground.

His head was down, keeping the wind out of his eyes. The rudder kept pushing at him and the tail wagged a bit, but he managed to keep hold. A glance through the rear window gave sight of Imogen lashing out at Mike with her left hand, followed by his vicious response. But that didn't stop her. Then she was using both fists, but still they raced on.

God knows what speed they were doing, but it was ridiculous. The engine was roaring in its efforts to drive them even faster. They were rapidly running out of runway, and the bushes beyond its end were ominously close. Something painful was about to happen.

The spinning propeller was a scythe to the fence. It cut the wire and wound it around itself like cotton on a reel, yanking lengths of it from the posts until it was so entangled the engine had no more strength and fell silent. Though the fence had snatched at the little Cessna, killing its speed, the vegetation beyond proved a better brake.

Cuff had only been able to cling to the leading edge of the tailplane. As the light aircraft charged into the bushes, he was thrown forward and into the trailing edge of the main wing, doubling him over. He fell off, winded, and struggled to get to his feet.

Mike clambered out. Cuff was on his hands and knees, wheezing in noisy attempts to suck air into his lungs. Mike kicked the gasping man over onto his back and knelt, banging his knees hard onto the heaving chest. Cuff looked up into a wild, bloodied face with swollen lips. Furious, vengeful blows rained down, and with them the memory of a schoolboy fight: on his back, Barry Castle's head and shoulders blocking out the sky above him, his massive fist poised.

Imogen came into his vision behind Mike. She locked an arm round his neck and hurled him backwards. He jumped up and punched her full in the face, once, twice. She staggered one step back and slumped to the ground.

The fire truck skidded to a halt. Craig, Jimmy and two students ran over. Cuff was on all fours and getting to his feet, aware of Mike heading back to him. But lanky, strong Craig locked his arm round the short man's neck and kept his little fighting feet off the ground.

Cuff struggled to stand. Still doubled over, wheezing painfully, his breath gradually returned. He stood up straight and looked around. Imogen was flat out on the grass. Her face was a mess, swollen and bleeding, Was she alive? *She's breathing.* The only thing he could do was turn her onto her side in the recovery position; the rest would be up to the paramedics.

Mike was now sitting on the Cessna's wheel, his head in his hands while Craig stood guard beside him.

'You little shit, Mike. What gives you the right to stuff up another person's life?'

Gripping his shirt front, Cuff yanked Mike to his feet. The flash of defiance in the little man's face evaporated immediately and he dropped his eyes. Blood watered by tears streaked his face and dripped onto his white shirt. One two-bar epaulette was missing, the other torn.

Nearby, Imogen moaned. Cuff could not help himself. He swung his whole body into the blow. An audible crunch, a bright red spray, and Mike's head whipped back against the Cessna. He sobbed. It was pitiful.

'You've been flying immigrants at night, haven't you? And you tried to blame me, didn't you?'

Mike gave a weak nod and a whimper as he cupped a hand over his nose, as if it would protect it or ease the pain. It was streaming freely. 'Yeah, it'll come out soon anyways. I didn't pay her.'

'What the hell are you talking about? You've also been stalking Imogen, haven't you. You really are an unpleasant little shit crying out for attention.'

Mike at last looked up to meet Cuff's glare. He stared over the fingers of his protective hand, uncomprehending. His nose broken and blocked, his voice distorted, he could only murmur. 'Stalking? Uh, uh. Not me. Trafficking yeah, but I ain't been stalking.'

'Then we still have another bastard out there.'

A siren heralded an ambulance tearing down the runway. Paramedics ran to the only prone person first, Imogen, who was trying to sit up. Police followed. Brief statements were taken from Cuff, Craig and Jimmy and the two students, who were both on their mobile phones. The police took Mike away. He went without resistance, head bowed, defeated and shamed. Imogen left in the ambulance. As the vehicle's doors shut her from Cuff's view, her hand flapped a wave at him.

They ended up in the Accident & Emergency unit. Cuff had to wait for an hour and a half and was then discharged after having his face cleaned and his arm dressed – it was bleeding again. Mike, who sat in the opposite corner of the room, did not have to wait long before he was seen, presumably because the uniformed police constable beside him made him a priority.

Occasionally Cuff stole a glance across the room, but never caught Mike looking his way. The man's head was down at one point, and he was using a handkerchief to dab at his eyes.

Cuff did nothing. There wasn't even anything to read. He spent his time studying the other casualties waiting there: a woman and her little girl who had bruises on her arms – questions were going to be asked about that, no doubt; a grey, pasty-faced man who looked to be at death's door – he was whisked away ahead of everyone else, even Mike; a drunk who kept dropping asleep onto his neighbour and once fell to the floor; and a man who was holding a blood-soaked cloth to his head and looking very sorry for himself. There were others, but these few provided enough material for Cuff to invent brief lives and stories behind their damaged exteriors.

Why had he risked his life? To cling to the tail of an aircraft at some insane speed and condemn it to a certain crash with no thought for his own safety was idiotic. There had been a desperation in his actions which was even greater than when he tried to stop Castle from falling to his death. He hadn't debated it, hadn't given it any thought at all. It was a purely instinctive act which he would not have taken but for Imogen. His cautious side had retreated; he was back to following his instincts. It was a comfortable feeling.

Released, he left the unit. He searched for Mike, but he had been taken away. Imogen was being held in for observation as she had been unconscious before the ambulance arrived.

Cuff tested her capacity for humour. 'I hope you're feeling better than you look.'

Her mouth twitched slightly. 'You're not exactly ready to have a portrait taken yourself. I feel okay, just bruised, but I'm having difficulty accepting what happened.'

'I examined myself in the bathroom mirror and, if it's any consolation, apart from the fact you are a hell of a lot prettier than I am to start with, we look much the same. Two black eyes each, both severely bloodshot, and cut and swollen lips. I might have a few more cuts and scratches than you due to certain bushes. But you'll be pleased to know the damage you inflicted on Mike is much the same as ours – well done.'

Her hands were resting on her tummy. He reached and

picked up the left one, examined it. It was bruised and swollen. 'That must be sore.'

He relaxed his hold, but she kept a weak grip on his fingers. 'I was hitting his face with the back of my hand, it was all I could do. If I'd had a weapon …'

'I saw you through the rear window.'

Imogen shook her head with a lack of comprehension. 'What on earth was he doing?'

Before Cuff could reply, a Detective Constable Wiley entered the ward and interrupted, requesting full statements from them. As part of his, Cuff produced Mike's supposed suicide note. The DC read it and said he wanted to keep it. Cuff showed it to Imogen first. 'I think it's self-explanatory, except for what he's done.'

'He's been stalking me, of course. The little, little … shit! I can't believe he was taking me along to kill me. I can't fathom it out.'

'No, I don't think so. He's admitted being guilty of trafficking, but I believed him when he said he hadn't been stalking. We're still looking for that man.'

'Oh God! No … I'm not so sure. Mike's such a liar. These trafficking flights would boost his ego; he did them well, landing by moonlight and so on. Stalking is creepy, it's not something he could boast about or be proud of. It would do nothing for his self-esteem, and he would deny it to others. It could still be him. If the messages stop now he's under arrest, that'll prove it.'

DC Wiley was obviously puzzled, but it was not what he had come to deal with, so he left, assuring them Mike was being interviewed at the station. Melissa, who had driven like hell to get there as soon as she received Cuff's message, came in as the policeman left. She stood two steps in from the doorway and regarded the two of them. She arched one eyebrow. 'Domestic already?'

Cuff stood to give Melissa the chair, but she motioned him down. 'Stay,' she said, 'you belong there.'

'Now is not the time for more matchmaking, Melissa.'

'Now is exactly the time. When are you two going to wake up to each other?'

Embarrassed, Cuff shook his head and mumbled, 'It's not as easy as you think.'

Imogen was smiling at her friend's manipulation. 'Cuff.'

'What?' His head was bowed; he didn't want to look at her or Melissa.

'Come here.' Imogen reached for his hand and pulled him closer. She grabbed his collar and pulled his head to hers. Their foreheads touched. Very gently, tender, bruised and split lips met.

'Thank you for saving me,' she whispered.

Melissa was grinning happily with her apparent success. 'Thank God for that. At last.'

Cuff sat again, releasing his hold on Imogen's hand. 'We need to get you back for a proper skills test as soon as possible.'

'Mmmh. There was definitely something wrong with me. I don't know what, but I'll bloody well pass it next time.'

'A hundred per cent.'

'A hundred per cent,' she laughed, keeping her lips tight to avoid opening the split.

'What on earth induced you to fly with that idiot?' Cuff asked. He studied Imogen's face. A range of expressions crossed it: embarrassment, frustration, anger at Mike, even herself maybe. Her mouth was pursed into that curious little circular shape she adopted when cross.

'It's complicated. He's got something over me,' was all she was prepared to say.

20

'I want Mike's camera.'

'Why?'

'There's stuff on it I need.'

Whatever the pictures were, Cuff knew they must be something he definitely did not want to see, or even know about. 'He's got something over me.' Imogen had said in the hospital.

'He's sleeping unhappily in a cell at the moment, there's no chance of being disturbed. So do you want to search his flat?'

'Can we get in?'

Cuff was amused at the nature of her response. It was not 'We can't do that, it's burglary', or 'It wouldn't be right'. No, her reply was 'How?'

'Easy. The locks are simple, and you can use a credit card

to prise the latch back. I've had to do it twice with mine when I forgot my keys. We'll get Melissa to keep watch. Wear gloves.'

'No. Melissa comes with me, you keep watch.'

Cuff shrugged. He opened Mike's flat door for them and went back across the road to Imogen's room, from where he could see the front entrance to the building, and waited.

The two women returned in less than fifteen minutes. Imogen was carrying a tin.

'Okay?' Cuff asked.

'Done, thank you. I've been thinking about my terrible skills test till my head hurts, and the only thing different that day from any other was the biscuits Mike gave me.' She held out the tin. 'Here, have one.'

Cuff stared at her, as a seed of understanding sprouted. 'No, I'll pass this time, thanks. What do you think?'

'Melissa has more experience than me. She reckons they could be made from cannabis.'

'Bastard! Your success and my reputation destroyed so easily.'

'Yes – bastard. The lying, deceiving son-of-a-bitch bastard! God, I'd love to hammer his smug, arrogant face again.' She took a deep breath. 'The good thing is now I know there was a foreign cause, I have much more confidence about my second test.'

'You don't have to lose an ounce of sleep over that.'

'Anyway, that's history now; back to the present. Look what came in while we were over there.' Imogen passed him her phone.

'With me you will be very happy, both emotionally and physically. Be prepared for a liberating physical relationship of endless experiments and satisfaction.'

'So he's still there, and it can't be Mike.'

'So sorry, Mike.' Imogen accentuated her sarcasm. 'There's

also one from Mr Hyde.'

'*You have not repented. Facebook, Flikr and Twitter are ready to launch. Social media infiltrates the world. Disgrace and shame will ruin your future.*'

Amongst the day's mail, which was unusually large, was a hand-delivered white envelope of a size which would suit a gift card. A single capital 'I' was written on the front. Imogen dreaded opening it, fearful of what it might say. Was it another threat, another obscene comment?

Since the previous full moon, which had clouded over, the number of text messages she had received had dropped to roughly one every other day, but their tone did not change. There was no escalation of the sexual innuendo, no explicit sexual remarks, no increase in the level of threats – they were all in the same vein: mend your ways or …

Still wary and still frightened of the eventual outcome should this man lose his self-control, Imogen was becoming inured to the onslaught. The texts no longer alarmed her, each one on its own; it was the continual presence of a man who was watching her, had desires on her and might indeed be dangerous that worried her. She was grateful for Melissa's presence in the flat and for Cuff's support. The two of them gave her a sense of security she trusted, although she was aware it could prove fragile if they let their guard slip.

After she had put off the inevitable by first dealing with all the other mail – the electricity and water bills, the charity request and the fourth catalogue of the month – she slit the envelope and pulled out a small piece of paper which didn't even need to be folded. The handwriting was almost illegible, the letters lacking any uniformity of height or length, as if an insect had trawled ink across the page: '*I know who is stalking you. Do not do anything. I will stop him.*'

Melissa arrived home and Cuff came over from across the

road armed with a bottle of wine. Imogen showed them the note. 'I don't recognise the writing, do you, Cuff?'

'No. It's distinctive enough, but we rarely see people's handwriting.'

'What's it telling us?' Melissa said. 'What is this person going to do about it?'

'I'm glad someone knows who he is, but what difference does it make to us now? We still need to go ahead with our plan. Do you agree?'

Soon it will be time to call her. I'm on edge – what will she reply? Have I attracted her sufficiently? If she succumbs, what am I going to do? I have planned for this moment for so long, but have not thought how the final act is going to be played. A candlelit dinner for two at my home, a passionate time in her room or mine? I must think before I call. She'll want an answer and swift action, or she'll cool.

Am I up to this? Suddenly I'm scared!

An earlier evening shower had left puddles on the road and the pavement. They reflected the orange street lights, which had just come on. A cat patrolled; silent paws on the wet tarmac. A neighbour rumbled his wheelie bin away. Imogen stopped staring out of the window and faced the room. Cuff had removed the cork from a bottle of wine and was placing some glasses on the counter-top.

'White?' he asked, and served Ginny and Melissa – the first to raise their hands. 'Red's coming up. Not you, Martin, you get too pissed and will fall over in the heat of the action.'

'I demand my rightful share. You have no right to deny me my rights.'

'Oh all right.' Cuff laughed and poured Merlot into three more glasses.

They waited. Martin said, 'What did this creep actually say,

Imogen?'

She did not answer, but put her glass down, unlocked her phone and showed it to him.

'*He will release your photos very soon. Only I can protect you from this, my love. What choice do you have, but to come to me? I will call you tonight.*'

'He doesn't say what time.'

Imogen took another sip of her drink. 'He once called me every half hour from three o'clock through to dawn. So who knows?'

'Do you think he really will call?'

Melissa didn't look up from picking fluff off her jeans. 'He will. This is a very organised man, a man who takes the trouble to send grammatically correct texts. I can't tell you what time, but he will call.'

'Nothing is going to happen tonight,' Cuff said. 'Imogen can tell us what happens tomorrow, so if you want to go home, nothing will be lost.'

'I'm very comfortable here, and I'm very interested.' Ginny wriggled further into the chair she was sharing with Martin.

Imogen walked up and down the room, which meant five steps around the furniture in one direction before turning to go back. Melissa stood and put an arm round her friend's shoulder. 'There's no need to be nervous, Imo. As Cuff says, nothing's going to happen tonight.'

'I'm not scared of tonight; my friends are here with me. I'm worried I'll fluff what I'm going to say, that he'll see through it.'

Her phone trumpeted its novel signal. Startled out of her worry, she jumped and rushed over to the kitchen counter to grab it.

'Shh, everyone.' Melissa put a finger to her lips.

'Hello,' Imogen said and hesitated. 'Hello?'

There was no answer. She had to lead him. 'Hello. I'm glad

you called. I wanted to tell you how much I love those pictures. You're very good, aren't you? I'm lucky, I have a good body, and you've done it more than justice through your clever use of shadows and highlights. You accentuated my curves brilliantly. You've shown me as more beautiful than I am, and I love that. Hello, are you still there?'

'Mmh.'

'Will you take more pictures of me please?'

The voice was croaky, the word drawn out and from the back of the throat – Marlon Brando in *The Godfather* sprang to her mind. 'Ye-es.'

'The last time was during the full moon. It shone in my window, and I was revelling in the sensation of being naked in its silvery light. You captured me so well. It's a full moon tomorrow, but it will still be bright for a few days, and the forecast is good for the next week. But let's make it tomorrow at midnight?'

'Ye-es.'

'Thank you so much. I didn't know you were there last time, but tomorrow I'll do something extra special for you to focus on. Wait – please. Before you go: why did you go away when you followed me and I turned back to meet you?'

The reply was short breathing.

Her voice was soft and purring. 'Okay, until tomorrow. Bye.'

She wants me to take more photos. This is a giant leap forward from frightened kitten to the cat rubbing against my leg. It was my skill in capturing her beauty in the shadows which did it. She is offering me her body for more – how can I deny her?

But is this a trap? A voice in my head tells me to stop this, but she is so beautiful and I need her so badly, and a stronger voice reminds me of the reward from continuing. What if I just take photos and stop the texts and stop him threatening her? Won't that settle her and increase her confidence in me? She knows he can be violent, he doesn't need to show her again. Sweetness and appreciation are what she wants, and I can give them to her using my photos as a channel.

What shall I do? Who shall I listen to?

Craig was leaning over Imogen again. Amused, Cuff watched his progress.

'Imogen, there's something about yellowed black eyes which turns me on.'

Imogen laughed and made to move away.

'Wait. Imogen, say after me: Craig.'

'Craig,' she repeated.

'You are a really super guy.'

'You are a really super guy.'

'And I would love to have a romantic dinner with you.'

Imogen tittered. 'And I would love to have a romantic dinner with you – but I'm not going to.'

'No, you had that bit wrong. Let's try again.'

She pushed him back and stood up straight. 'Craig, I have my skills test in ten minutes. That's more important to me than any man. Do. You. Under. Stand?'

'You'll change your mind one day, Imo, and you'll be forever grateful for my persistence. And you'll sail through this test, Cuff told me so, eh Cuff?'

'I did, and you will.'

Connor came out of his office. 'Are you ready, Imogen?'

'Coming, Connor.' Clutching her headset and maps folder, she followed him out of the crew room with a quick backward glance.

Cuff looked at Craig, Sonia and Jimmy, who had joined them. 'She'll be fine. We think we know what was wrong with her last time.'

'Weed?' Sonia asked.

'Yes, but not intentionally, especially when she knew she was taking a test. Mike gave her some biscuits before the flight.'

'That man! I thought she had likely symptoms.'

'How do you know? Shared the odd joint, Sonia?' Jimmy teased.

She punched his arm. 'Don't be cheeky. Only in my youth, and only a little bit. Seriously, from the way she was acting and what she experienced, it's possible. It affects people in different ways.'

Two and a half hours later, Connor strode into the crew room with his usual noncommittal expression, from which no one could gain any clues as to the result. Imogen followed. The question was there on everyone's faces, but she shrugged her shoulders and turned into Connor's office for her debrief. Cuff, as her instructor, knocked and joined them.

21

15 September

Sonia's tiny flat was a mess. She knew it, but could never be bothered to do anything about it. No one visited her, which meant no one else ever saw it. But now Jimmy was coming round, so she'd better do something. It didn't need to be a deep clean, because she had a pretty good idea Jimmy's home was an equal mess. He was a shambolic creature, even if he was rather nice.

What was wanted was a cleaning witch.

The bedroom: dirty washing, smelly running shoes, other junk. Dump it all in the cupboard, make the bed.

Why was she worried about her bedroom? Jimmy wasn't going to go in there – or was he? She gave a brief and amused snort at her imagination – you never know.

The kitchen. *The bloody kitchen, I'll have to do something.* She did, and it was brutal.

Time was running out. It was already eight o'clock and he would be there soon.

Jimmy was late. He was always late, but one would have thought, for a date like this, one which could lead to anything, he would try to be on time. Sonia was a little irked and worried he had chickened out, but he knocked at half past and stood on the step, back from the door, with a six-pack of beer and a bottle of plonk in his hands.

In spite of his grin, he looked nervous. But the alcohol worked its magic, and choosing what they wanted to order from the takeaway curry menu got things going. The food came. Sonia paid, Jimmy put in half and, meal over, paper plates and foil containers strewn everywhere, they settled back to finish the wine. Simultaneously they suppressed burps, and laughed easily at each other. Things were progressing nicely in a direction Sonia had previously been uncertain she wanted.

The single table lamp did little to light the flat. The curtains were closed but for a slit between them, letting the moonlight cast a narrow beam of brilliance which tracked slowly round the room. Both of them had watched as it picked out the half-finished punnet of dhal, discarded it as worthless and progressed to Jimmy's prawn vindaloo, and then Sonia's lamb sag.

'You left a piece of meat there.' Jimmy pointed to a highlighted brown chunk in the corner of the container.

'I couldn't eat another thing. Curry does that to me. I'll have to run it off in the morning.'

'The moon's bright tonight and full. Must be cheese.'

'It's full? Oh my God!' Sonia's fingers reached for her mouth.

'What? Are you okay?' Jimmy's hand went out to her. She clutched it in both of hers.

'It's going to happen!' She was staring at him and still squeezing his hand.

'What?'

'Jimmy, I'm so sorry, I've got to go. I don't want to, but I've got to. I'll talk to you tomorrow.' Rushing, she retrieved her trainers from the bedroom cupboard and slipped them on. Without concern for what he saw, she stripped off her shirt, revealing her skinny frame and unrestrained breasts, and dived into a track top. Turfing all the washing out of the cupboard, she found a floppy hat and tucked it in her waistband. She shooed him out the door and ran off along the road, looking back once. He had slumped down onto the step, looking like a puppy deprived of its treat. She blew him a kiss and accelerated.

'This man hacks me off. We should be celebrating my success this morning, not preparing for battle.'

'She was dancing round the crew room after the debrief. It was quite a sight,' Cuff told the others. 'Celebrations for England winning the World Cup in rugby and football, having a Wimbledon champion and coming first in the Round the World yacht race would have nothing on that performance.'

'Don't mock me, it means a lot.'

Martin raised his glass. 'We can still celebrate, Imogen, it's a while to midnight.'

'There'll be time enough for celebrations later. Hopefully it will be a double one, with Imogen's pass and the stalker caught. Then you can get pissed, Martin. Now, we stay sober.' Cuff stood and paced about. 'All right everyone, let's run through it. Ginny, you're going into the other room in the dark where you can't be seen and watch the roof opposite with these binoculars. If you see activity, you tell me. He's supposed to materialise at midnight, so let's open a call at a quarter to and wait. I reckon he's got to set up a tripod or some sort of rest in order to hold a heavy camera and lens still enough for a decent exposure at night.

'Imogen and Melissa, you two are going to strip off and let your forms be lit by the moonlight. It's not our business what you show our stalker. Martin, you and I are going back to my flat where we'll wait for Ginny to call. If she sees the stalker on the roof, we'll rush up there via the roof ladder at the back and corner him, okay?'

'No.' Imogen stepped forward. 'I'm coming with you. I want to be there when you get him, I want to be in at the kill. Melissa has agreed to pose alone for our man, and he's not going to tell the difference in the moonlight.'

'O-kay,' Cuff said, dragging the word out, 'but we will be on the roof, so there's always the danger of slipping and falling.'

'The same danger applies to you – why should I be different? Because I'm a woman? Don't even think of saying that. I'm coming with you.'

Melissa was grinning. 'That's told you. Now listen, you two.' She pointed at the men. 'I'm stripping for the stalker to take his photos. I'm not giving you a peep show, so you bloody well keep your eyes somewhere else. This is not for your benefit.'

'One word, Martin, one word on Melissa and I'll take you apart!' Ginny laughed, wagging her finger at him.

It was a quarter to twelve and Sonia was racing down the street. At the beginning of the block she slowed to a walk, using it to catch her breath; sprinting was not her strength. Pulling her hood up, she forced the hat on top and walked on with slow, uncertain steps and bent over, hoping she resembled an old lady – *in trousers, for God's sake? Will it fool him?*

The front door of the house was unlocked. Up the stairs, she found Imogen's flat and hammered on the door.

A fair-haired woman in a dressing gown stood there. She looked annoyed.

Sonia burst past her into the room. 'Where's Imogen?'

'Who the hell are you?'

Another voice came from the next room. 'Cuff, he's there. Melissa, go for it!'

The blonde shed her gown in one easy movement and stepped gracefully into the moonlight. 'Imogen's across the road, and we're doing something. Don't interrupt. In fact, get out of here!'

'Oh God! What's going on? What are you doing?'

The voice from the other room said, 'He's crouching down, he must be looking through his camera.'

Sonia tore off her top. She cupped her hands under her little breasts, pushing them up and forward and shoved in front of Melissa to the window, exposing her torso to the entire street.

Cuff bolted out of the room and to the fire exit. Martin was on his heels, but Imogen elbowed herself ahead of him. The only way to the roof was via the fire escape. There was no need for speed now; the stalker was trapped above them. They padded quietly up the short flight of stairs. The door at the top was normally locked, but was now ajar. Its rusty hinges had been oiled and gave no shrieks of pain. It led onto an iron landing on the outside of the building with a ladder to the roof, whose six metal rungs sang muted notes at every step.

They crouched to form a tight group on the narrow gutter which surrounded the pitched roof, separating it from the parapet. This level section was barely wide enough to walk on. To move along it, one foot had to be lifted past the tiles of the pitched section to put it down directly in front of the other. It was not an area for fast movement.

They bent low to keep out of sight below the ridgeline. Cuff ushered Martin round the roof to the right, while he went left to trap the stalker in a pincer movement. He knew he could not keep Imogen out of this, and the best thing was for her to add her strength to his short friend's. But he pulled her in behind him; she'd be better protected there.

Martin made his way along the back edge of the building and cautiously round the corner at its end. He gave Cuff a thumbs up as he reached the far end of the roof and crept on.

The idea was for Martin to appear first to the photographer, so the man would turn and escape the other way, straight into Cuff who was hiding at his end of the building.

Cuff and Imogen snuck forward to their front corner and crouched. Martin came into view again, now above the front windows.

Between them was the dim shape of a hooded person with his backside on the pitched roof and his feet in the gutter. His torso was bent low behind the indistinct lump of his camera, which rested on the waist-high balustrade which formed the parapet. The man, totally absorbed in his task, had not yet noticed Martin.

Cuff glanced across the road. *What on earth …?*

The photographer swore. His camera scraped against stone as he carelessly picked it off the ledge. His slow movement spelled despondency as he rose to his feet. He turned to leave but, as he did so, glanced back. The sight of Martin so close must have shaken him. He froze, but only for a moment. The next he was hurrying along the gutter, one hand on the parapet, the other held out to keep balance and stop himself falling inward to the pitched roof.

The stalker was almost at the corner – only the end of the building and a few steps to go to reach the fire escape remained before he could run. Cuff stood upright, Imogen behind him. They were two yards away.

He had little option, with one person behind him and two in front. He turned on Martin. 'Get out of my way.'

Martin stood his ground. The stalker glanced back – Cuff was closing on him. One choice was left. He clambered onto the pitched roof to cross directly over the top to the fire ladder. Cuff jumped after him, caught a heel and dragged him slithering back down the tiles. The man struggled and hit out. They wrestled, their feet confined in the narrow gutter. Martin grabbed the man from behind, but he fought with the fury of the possessed. Martin was too small to win. Imogen scrambled up onto the tiles to get past Cuff to help. She slid down feet first and kicked the man in his belly. He grunted and lashed sideways at her. She grabbed his arm and hung on.

With Martin on his back, Cuff trying to subdue him and Imogen hanging on to his left arm, the stalker was losing, but he was keeping them busy. He wasn't giving up.

No one quite knew how it happened, but suddenly the man was falling back over the parapet. He screamed and grasped at the stone. His grip failed.

Cuff caught one hand, the other was flailing desperately for a hold. Cuff managed to catch that too.

Time slowed. Cuff was back there on the cliff. He was gripping Barry Castle's sweaty arms as the man wriggled in his desperation. His inexorable slide to the rocks a hundred feet below, dragging Cuff with him, was his fate. Castle's face, contorted by panic and fear, was crying, pleading with him yet again as it had so often in his dreams these past few months.

Cuff held on. The pain from his dog-savaged arm almost overwhelmed him, and once again the sweat lubricated his grip as the stalker struggled.

No, it wasn't going to happen again. This time, he was not being pulled to his own death, and he didn't have to let go to save himself. He would be a rescuer. And this time, it wasn't Castle.

The camera had somehow swung round to the photographer's back, so the strap was across his throat. A detail which imprinted itself in Cuff's mind as he used all his strength to pull the stalker up. The man was too heavy, but Martin took a grip on his left arm, and Imogen came from off the tiles to help.

Together they hauled Connor to safety.

22

16, 19 September

They were all going to be there, all who had been involved in Connor's capture the previous night. Arriving at the Red Lion, the closest pub to the airfield, at almost the same time were Imogen, Melissa and Cuff. As they walked together through the bar to the garden, a tattooed man at the counter looked at their fading yellow facial bruises and said cheerfully, 'Looks like she gave you as good as she got, eh, mate?'

Another drinker further along laughed as well. 'Made up now though, 'ave we?'

They couldn't be annoyed at the ragging. Cuff grinned at them. 'She's tough to beat. Got to respect that.'

Imogen raised a fist in the air. 'He won't try again in a hurry.' She meant Mike.

There were four picnic tables outside in the sun, each of which could seat six – eight with a squeeze. Cuff returned from the bar with their drinks.

'I think I'm on a bit of a high after last night,' Imogen said. 'That fight on the roof top and then rescuing Connor set my adrenalin pumping. There's a part of me wants more thrills like that. I think I was more scared in the woods last month, but I felt like this afterwards as well. Am I weird?'

Melissa laughed. 'Without doubt.'

Cuff said, 'I'm just the same. I used to take plenty of risks, calculated ones, purely to experience the thrill. Then I decided I had to live a more stable life if I wanted to be well off and wallow in luxury in my old age. I tried hard to settle down, but it doesn't work for me. Trouble seeks me out, and the problem is I really enjoy living the danger – I get huge satisfaction from overcoming my fears. I need excitement and risk to function, to be happy.'

Imogen was watching his face. His words brought him closer, somehow. 'Ginny warned me about you, about being dragged into your harebrained schemes, remember?'

'Ginny fusses too much. It worked, though, didn't it?'

'It did.' There was a warmth in Cuff's close presence. She suppressed it, it was too soon. She had said 'Thank you for saving me' in the hospital, but was that really why she'd kissed him? In any case, he had withdrawn his hand from hers afterwards. He could have let it linger there, but he didn't. So he wasn't ready either.

Her friend dug her in the ribs and gave her a mischievous grin. Melissa was on a matching mission again. Imogen was about to tell her to stop interfering in her business, when Ginny and Martin arrived.

Sonia joined them. She was the one who had asked them to come before they disbanded in the early hours of Tuesday, saying she had something to discuss. But she emphasised that the only person who could make a decision about it was Imogen.

When the whole group were settled with their drinks, Sonia began. 'I've asked you all here because a lot is at stake for the flying school now Connor has been exposed for what he is. I hope before we go home this afternoon we can hear what decision Imogen has made and what she wants to do. If there's anyone here who will not be able to keep these discussions and their outcome secret – I mean, never disclose them to anyone – please leave now. If you stay, I trust you'll agree to say nothing to anyone else.'

They all agreed, verbally or by positive head movements, and nobody got up to leave.

'First, I have to make clear I'm now an equal partner with Connor in the school. Effectively, given what's happened, I'll be running things for some time to come. I think Connor will be too embarrassed to show himself in public and is likely to take a back seat for a while, talking only to me. Of course, what actually happens is down to what Imogen decides.'

Sonia went on to explain how many students were dependent on the school. She said their money would be wasted and their flying careers put back if it became known that Connor had gone through an 'episode of perversion', as she put it. She told them how she and Connor had been an item years ago and it had continued sporadically since. Because of this she had discovered what he was doing by looking at the photos on his camera and later at messages on a phone she didn't know he had.

'If you ask me why he did it, I would say Connor never had any real affection in his life. There was never a genuine spark between us. My guess is his imagination told him he could have a woman love him if he owned her.'

'I can tell you why.' Imogen opened a folded piece of paper. 'He wrote me this letter. I won't bore you with the first part, it's all about how much he loves me and what a wonderful life he'll have with me if I'll go to him. But at the end of that part is a clear warning: "Otherwise …", and it's what follows that's pertinent.' She stood and glanced at the group of faces: all serious, all curious and all concerned.

'There is another man. I know him. He had a deep love once. To see her was to witness pure beauty. He worshipped her, but she betrayed him. Not once or twice, but with three different men. She laughed in his face and embarrassed him in public about deeply personal things. He was wounded. She destroyed his self-esteem, and he learned to hate. Eventually, he began to rebuild his life and found other women, but they were all shallow. There was another, but she too was so flawed he could not live with her.'

Imogen paused to take a breath. Sonia flinched and looked away.

'More recently he saw you. You are perfect. You remind him of his first unfaithful love, for whom he has an undying hatred. Because of her, he does not like perfect women, he sees them as a threat, and so he means to harm you. Unfairly, he seeks revenge on all women. His beliefs are so ingrained in his psyche I cannot change this man. The only way I can protect you is for you to come to me. Once he sees the perfect woman has submitted herself to me, he will turn his attention elsewhere, knowing you are beyond his reach.

Do not take the threat he presents lightly, Imo. He means you very real harm. I don't think he would go so far as to kill you, but he will want to ensure your perfection is ruined, disfigured so no man will want you and you will die a lonely spinster in your allotted time.

I'm extending my hand of succour, friendship and love to you. You who have been sent by God to accompany me through life. I desperately want to save you — let me. I could not live a moment longer if I failed and you were condemned to live the rest of your life in painful disfigurement and the misery of loneliness.

Come to me Imo, my love. Soon I will contact you on how we do this. Until then I will protect you, but if he sees my efforts are failing … I cannot say what he will do or when he will act — but he will.'

Imogen put the letter down and took a drink. 'There you have it. Betrayed, 'wounded', and so he becomes misogynistic. Sonia?'

'I didn't know about the woman he lost. It must have been twenty or so years ago. We've talked about the two character types he used. He knows exactly what he did – he's clear that he invented the threatening one to try to frighten you into going to him. He also knew he had to stop after I confronted him, and he promised he would, but after that the wrong voice in his head had the last say.'

Cuff put up his hand to interrupt her. 'Why did you rush into Imogen's flat and ruin Connor's photos?'

Sonia snorted a short laugh at the recollection. 'I told you the school is the most important thing in this saga. It must be kept going, and I really wanted to avoid a scandal. I had a strong feeling you guys were going to trap him somehow, so I first of all sent you a note asking you to leave him to me. I didn't hold out much hope that would put you off, so I tried to warn him before you got to the roof. He would see me and not Imogen and know the game was up. I was too late.'

Melissa laughed. 'It was quite funny in retrospect. You and I fighting for front position to reveal our naked bodies to the world.'

Sonia chuckled. 'I suppose so. There was a point when I almost exposed him, but I felt more good would come from my gaining some influence in the school than from bringing the place down. You might think that was selfish of me, but my life is in that school. I have invested so much time and effort in making it something to be proud of, I couldn't see it collapse. That's why I believe I was absolutely right to force Connor into making me a partner. Call it blackmail if you will, but I did it for the good of the school, not for money. Aside from that, I don't think anything will be gained by reporting him. I think he's so shocked and ashamed by what he's done he will never stalk anyone again.'

She sat and took a large draught of beer, glanced briefly at Imogen and studied the tabletop in front of her.

Imogen waited a long time to answer. She took several sips from her glass while everyone else waited patiently. 'Do you believe he's genuinely sorry?'

'Yes, I think he's deeply ashamed, I really do.'

'Is he genuinely ashamed, or is he feeling sorry for himself and dreading being reported?'

'Probably both. But Imogen, he's genuinely ashamed. I know him. I've never seen him broken before, and it's going to be very difficult for him to hold his head up, even if nobody else knows anything about this.'

Again Imogen remained silent for a while before answering. 'I want to get on with my life. My course is over, and I can now get my licence. I need to progress rapidly to get into an airline, and I want to do that and build up my hours here at Fernbury. In spite of everything, I'm comfortable here.'

She paused, then sipped her drink again. She stared up into the overhanging tree; there were so many branches, leaves and catkins, as well as insects and birds that depended on the great trunk – and the trunk depended on them. *Isn't that the same with us? The lesser depending on the greater, and the greater living off the lesser. The school needs us and, in our different ways, we need the school.*

Aloud, Imogen said, 'For the school's benefit, for all our benefits, the least disruption the better. I'm not vindictive. Connor's had a massive effect on my life. He's had me confused, angry and scared, but when confronted he backed down – twice. Plus, he's not the only person who's challenged me recently. I was under pressure from Mike at the same time, which compounded the effect on me. If I isolate what Connor did, I could have controlled his influence.

'As Sonia has said, there are more positives to dropping this than there are in having Connor charged. The police know there's a stalker, but they don't know who it is. If the harassment stops, they need never know. If it starts again, they will learn who it is. So I won't report him to the police, but I do want time with him – in private. I need an explanation and an apology.'

'Thank you, Imogen, thank you. You won't regret that decision. Craig and Jimmy are inside, Cuff. Please call them out here. They need to hear this too.'

The two men perched on the end of the benches. There wasn't much room left, so Cuff stood next to Imogen.

Sonia took another gulp of beer. She appeared nervous to Cuff, taking her drink as Dutch courage. 'I have a confession and I have to tell you something that best comes from an authentic source – me – rather than hearing it bandied around the bar or in the paper. You all know Mike's been arrested for taking the Cessna 150 and abducting Imogen. What you may not know is there are several other counts, which include using the C172 for a few nights a month around the full moon, flying to somewhere in France and bringing illegal immigrants, Albanians, into the country.'

Sonia paused to let that sink in to those who weren't aware. 'What he may not have known, but I reckon he did, was these deluded people were enslaved by what the police believe is a gang of their own countrymen. The police are trying to trace them, but I was told they might struggle with that.'

Cuff interrupted. 'Mike knew. I'm sure of it. I saw him at a car wash talking to the foreign boss, and later Martin and I saw one of the migrants he smuggled at the same place. We chased but lost him. Mike tried to pin the theft of the aircraft on me. Did you know this all along, Sonia?'

She nodded. 'Affirmative. It was him I saw copying the aircraft keys one night. The foot brace was an alibi of sorts.

How could he fly with that support on? He never sprained his ankle, it was all a lie. Once I learned these flights were taking place, I put two and two together and confronted him. He confessed because I tried to blackmail him too. I admit it, I don't have a guilty conscience over that either.' She gave a short titter. 'Maybe I could make a career out of blackmail.'

'After the crash, when he was beaten and had just been arrested, he told me he hadn't paid up. Was it you he was referring to?'

'Must have been. He didn't pay, so I was going to go to the police. His attempted suicide negated all that.'

Cuff sat, managing to perch one cheek on the bench next to Imogen. She shifted a little to give him more room.

'I have more news.' Sonia's face was suddenly illuminated by a broader smile than any of them had ever seen from her before, one which instantly made her more attractive. 'Jimmy and I have decided to live together.'

'Brilliant!' Craig stood and raised his mug. 'Great news. Well done both of you and the very best of luck and skill in making a success of it. You'll need it with that bloke, Sonia!'

Imogen whispered, 'What do you think about Craig for Melissa?'

Cuff laughed. 'Go on then, get your own back. I don't think you'll have to try too hard. Watch.' Craig had stood and was standing over Melissa in his characteristic 'keep her penned in and subject her to my charm' mode.

Imogen's hand squeezed his under the table. 'Thank you for everything you've done.'

'Thanks are not necessary. It was an interesting experience, although a bit worrying at times. Now that you're a qualified pilot and out from under my influence, would you like to go out on Friday? It's my day off. Just the two of us.'

'I'll have to think about that – for half a second. Yes, let's. Where?'

* * *

A sunny day. A grassy slope above a quarry. A view for miles. A blanket in the shade. Cheese, chunky bread, pickles, strawberries and cream, and an ice-cold bottle of wine.

'This is a lovely spot. How did you find it?'

'This is where the twins tried to kill me, over the edge right there.' Cuff pointed.

'What a place to come back to! What made you choose it for today? It's suddenly become sinister.'

'I enjoy facing down my demons, and the police told me the twins have been arrested at the ferry terminal. I must admit, that's a worry put to rest. Wine?'

'Please.'

'The last time we lay on the ground together was not so comfortable.'

'A bit scary too, with that dog panting in my face.'

Ginny picked the grains from a piece of wholewheat bread and tossed them to The Gargoyle's swans. The group watched the hurried pecking and manoeuvring to snatch the last speck from the surface.

'Cuff, do you recall the conversation we had in June about the direction your life was taking? We were sitting right here.'

'Yes, I felt something was missing. You said it was a girlfriend.'

'And you denied it. You said it was excitement. Have you had your fill of that for a while?'

'I'm not sure I'll ever end my search for thrills, but I seem to have solved the girlfriend problem.' He put his arm round Imogen and pulled her closer. 'I hope she'll join me in the quest, or at least not object to a little risk.'

She smiled happily. 'She'll join you, and if you try to leave her behind you'll be in trouble. I've been scared, won through and found I've been rejuvenated each time. I rather like it.'

Martin said, 'You've reverted to the person you were before you got married and tried to be a businessman. We invented an alter ego for you – Jonathan – and as far as I'm concerned you've now become him. Back where you were before you made that fateful decision.'

'I agree. Cuff was short for Cuthbert, which you hated,' Ginny said, 'so you might as well become Jonathan and complete the transition. Being Cuff didn't work.'

'It goes to prove you can't change your basic nature, you can only change what you've learned. I made the wrong choice and suffered the consequences, but I feel I'm back to my true self now.'

Melissa raised her glass. 'To my dear friend Imogen and her man – Jonathan.'

* * *

Before You Go

Thank you for reading ***The Pilot***. I hope you enjoyed this series. If you did and have a moment to spare, writing a short review on Amazon, Goodreads or your favourite site would be greatly appreciated. Authors depend on reader opinions in order to produce enjoyable works. Reviews help authors to further their careers.

To find out more about the author and his works please visit:
https://www.helifish.co.uk where you have the option to subscribe to his mailing list.

You can also find him on Facebook: http://www.facebook.com/casole75
and on Twitter: @helifish74

I look forward to hearing from you.

Also by CA Sole

In ***Scott's Choice*** Cuthbert Jonathan Scott is a young man with a dominant adventurous spirit. He grew up being indoctrinated by his father into an approach to life that was completely at odds with his nature: take no risks, caution in everything, settle down while young, save your money, on and on. A random event results in a decisive moment. He is torn between two options: following his father's teaching or being himself.

Two personae emerge. One, Jonathan, begins a life following his natural instincts. His spirit of adventure predominates. His choice has consequences which bring several life-threatening events but also great rewards.

Jonathan's alter ego, Cuff, is the brainwashed youth who tries to adopt the more cautious approach. But his nature conflicts with this and leads him on a dangerous path to escape the mundane existence which was the consequence of his choice. It seems he cannot avoid risk. Indeed, danger appears to seek him out.

Two independent stories develop in ***Scott's Choice***. The tales are linked only by his friends and enemies who continue to influence and react to events in Cuff's life in one way, and in Jonathan's life in another. However, certain events are common to both and fixed in the calendar.

Nature's Justice is the first sequel to ***Scott's Choice***. It traces Jonathan's life as he and Gudrun experience a horrific event in Southern Africa. Witnesses to the killing of a rhino and the sighting of the person responsible for the trade in horns, they are chased and hounded over a thousand kilometres from the Kruger Park through South Africa and Botswana to the Victoria Falls.

#

A Fitting Revenge is a thriller about extraordinary events that happen to ordinary people.

Your friends are in deep trouble. What if you take a step too far in avenging them?

In southern rural England, Alastair is helping his close friend to avoid a punishing divorce from Sandra. But Sandra is ruthless, merciless and determined to win.

As Alastair is drawn into a situation which he battles to control, the love binding him and Juliet is ripped apart. With the common goal of rescuing their friend, they strive to work together, but the tension between them only widens the rift as Alastair faces the ruination of his life.

* * *

Fighting his way out of the turmoil, Alastair stretches reason to exact a terrible revenge for the extortion and assault that has affected his friends. In doing so, he discovers a side to himself which he never knew existed.

Revenge must be taken, but is Alastair's 'eye for an eye' concept too extreme? Will Juliet remain a love lost?

The Author

CA Sole began writing in 1990 with a thriller titled Zahak's Breath. An agent took it on and, after a few not insignificant changes, submitted it to a publisher. The first rejection dented his ego and left its mark! Colin took the extraordinary and foolish step of giving up his full-time job to write in 1995. His confidence took another hit, and he had to return to work for enough money to buy beer. He persevered, wrote a couple of short stories and about half a novel. That short manuscript has been incorporated into one of the sequels of the Scott series.

Colin's first published novel, *A Fitting Revenge*, came out in 2016 and quickly received 4- and 5-star reviews on Amazon and Goodreads. His second book, CJ, was done through a small publisher and also received a small number of 4- and 5-star reviews. However, Colin's lack of enthusiasm (and plain laziness) over marketing resulted in poor sales. CJ has been rewritten and published in the summer of 2019 as *Scott's*

Choice. It has two sequels: ***Nature's Justice*** and ***The Pilot***.

Having been in the British Army, a professional helicopter pilot and an aviation consultant, his work has taken him all over the world to some 66 countries. He lived and worked in Africa – North, South, East and West – for 43 years before returning to England for good. It's therefore not surprising that the background to Colin's books is travel.

There is far too much of the less trodden world left to see.

To find out more about CA Sole's works and future projects, please visit: https://www.helifish.co.uk